Also by Sandra Brown

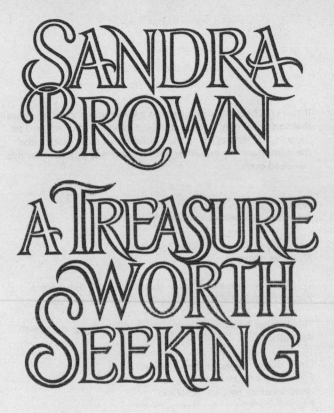

SANDRA BROWN

A TREASURE WORTH SEEKING

WARNER BOOKS

A Time Warner Company

WARNER BOOKS EDITION

This book was previously published under the pseudonym Rachel Ryan by Dell Publishing Company, Inc. in 1982.

This Warner Books Edition is published by arrangement with the author.

Cover design by Jackie Merri Meyer
Cover photo by Herman Estevez
Hand lettering by Carl Dellacroce

Warner Books, Inc.
1271 Avenue of the Americas
New York, NY 10020
Visit our Web site at
www.warnerbooks.com

W A Time Warner Company

Printed in the United States of America

First Warner Books Printing: September, 1992

20 19 18 17

To Vivian Stephens
with gratitude

Dear Reader,

For years before I began writing general fiction, I wrote genre romances under several pseudonyms. *A Treasure Worth Seeking* was originally published more than ten years ago (under my first pen name, Rachel Ryan).

This story reflects the trends and attitudes that were popular at that time, but its themes are eternal and universal. As in all romance fiction, the plot revolves around star-crossed lovers. There are moments of passion, anguish, and tenderness—all integral facets of falling in love.

I very much enjoyed writing romances. They're optimaistic in orientation and have a charm unique to any other form of fiction. If this is your first taste of it, please enjoy.

Sandra Brown

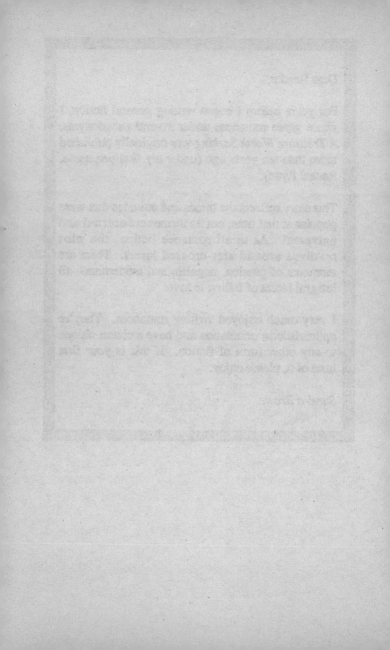

CHAPTER
One

In spite of the calm assurance she projected, Erin O'Shea was quaking with nervousness as she pressed the doorbell. She heard the chimes tolling within the interior of the house. It was an attractive house, situated in one of San Francisco's middle-class neighborhoods.

Glancing over her shoulder at the other houses lining the street, Erin reflected on the well-maintained neighborhood. The lawns were well kept; the houses, if not ostentatious, were immaculate and tasteful. The house she stood before was painted dove gray and accented with white trim. Like all the other houses on the street, it typified San Francisco's architecture, having the garage level with the street and the house elevated. Steep concrete steps led up to the front door, which boasted an old-fashioned etched glass window.

She tried to peer through the opaque glass and

glimpse some sign of movement as she listened for approaching footsteps, but could see nothing and heard no sounds from within the house.

What if no one were at home? Erin hadn't thought of that possibility. Indeed, she had thought of nothing since she had deplaned from the flight from Houston except finding this house. Her thoughts while navigating the picturesque streets of San Francisco had been single-minded and purposeful. Today was the culmination of a three-year search. She had prevailed over musty record books, endless long-distance telephone calls, slammed doors, and disappointing false leads to be standing here at this moment.

Today she would see her brother for the first time in her life. Today she would be face-to-face with her only blood relative.

Her heart lurched when she heard footsteps coming toward the door. His wife? A maid? *Her brother?* She swallowed hard.

The door was opened slowly. He stood in front of her. "Mr. Kenneth Lyman?" she asked.

He didn't answer her. Instead his eyes raked her from the top of her head to her toes. His rapid inspection couldn't have taken more than a fraction of a second, but she felt that he had missed nothing.

"Mr. Kenneth Lyman?" she repeated.

He nodded curtly.

All her nervousness fled and was replaced by immeasurable joy when the man confirmed that he was her brother. He was so handsome! She was surprised to find nothing in his features that resembled her. He was as fair as she was dark. Whenever she had tried to visualize him, she had conjured up a face that was a masculine version of her own, but this man was nothing like she expected.

His hair was sandy brown, but when only a glimmer of the weak February sunlight struck it, it shone golden. Perched atop the mussed strands was a pair of eyeglasses with narrow tortoiseshell frames. The eyebrows that bridged his wide forehead were thick and as golden as his hair. Blue eyes, which were scrutinizing her closely, were fringed by thick short lashes that were dark at the base and gilded at the ends.

His nose was straight and narrow. The mouth underneath it was firm, wide, almost stern. There was a beguiling vertical cleft in his strong chin that suggested a stubbornness of will.

"Forgive me for staring," she apologized even as she continued to look at him intently. Would she ever tire of seeing this face she had searched for for so long?

He still didn't say anything. His eyes darted behind her as if he expected to see someone accompanying her. They took in the white Mercedes she had rented at the airport, the house across the street, the entire surroundings in one sweeping glance before they came back to her. It was disconcerting that he hadn't said anything. But then, he didn't know who she was.

"I've come a long way to see you," she said

for a start. "May I come in and talk to you for a moment?"

"What do we have to talk about?"

Her heart was pierced by a sweet pain at the first sound of his deep, low-timbred voice. But the pleasure changed to shyness in deference to his harsh tone. He probably thought she was selling something. "I . . . well, it's rather personal." She didn't want to introduce herself to him while standing on the doorstep.

"Okay. You'd better come in." He moved aside and she took a tentative step through the front door. He glanced around the yard once more before closing the door and turning to face her.

Standing this close to him, she was made aware for the first time how tall he was. She was considered tall for a woman, and yet he seemed to tower over her. Or maybe it was his overbearing attitude. Her brother seemed to exude power and a commanding control. He wasn't muscle-bound, but radiated a strength that was intimidating.

Erin looked past the loosened knot of his necktie to the strong cords of his neck. The sleeves of his shirt had been rolled to his elbows to reveal tanned, sinewy forearms. The white cotton was stretched across a broad chest that tapered into a flat stomach, and his long legs were hard and lean beneath gray flannel slacks. Perhaps he played basketball. Tennis? Surely he was athletically inclined to have maintained this wiry physique. She knew him to be thirty-three.

He perpetuated the unnerving silence and stared at her with as much temerity as she was looking at him. When she shifted her handbag from her shoulder to under her arm, every muscle in his body tensed though he hadn't actually moved. He was like a cat about to pounce.

He isn't making this easy for me, Erin thought. Maybe he didn't want to know what had happened to the younger sister from whom he had been separated thirty years ago. Maybe he wasn't even aware he had a sister.

"My name is Erin O'Shea," she said by way of introduction.

"Miss O'Shea," he spoke her name in that same stirring voice. His blue eyes hadn't left her face. She moistened her drying lips with the tip of her tongue.

"May I sit down somewhere?" she asked.

With an outstretched hand he indicated a room to the left of the entrance hall and she walked toward it. She assessed the comfortable furnishings of the house. It was tastefully, though not expensively, decorated. Somehow the interior of the house didn't coincide with her first impressions of her brother. She thought he would have leaned toward a more austere decor to match his taciturn personality.

What was she doing? She hadn't been with him for more than a few minutes, and she was already analyzing his psyche! Still, the house, this room where she was taking a seat on a splashy sofa, didn't seem to fit the man. Most likely his wife had decorated the house.

"Is Melanie at home?" she asked politely.

His answer was slow and careful. "No. She had to go out."

Erin smiled and relaxed somewhat. She was glad that they would have some time alone. Having an audience when she identified herself might make them both uncomfortable. "Now that I think about it, I'm surprised to find you at home in the middle of a weekday. I would have thought you'd be at the bank." She knew her brother was a banker.

The eyes he had narrowed on her now shifted to her brown suede purse, which she had placed beside her on the sofa. He had a way of making one feel that he hadn't missed a movement. "I came home early today," was his only reply.

"Kenneth—may I call you Kenneth?" At his nod, she continued. The time had come. "Kenneth, what I'm going to tell you will surprise you." She laughed nervously. "Maybe *shock* is a better word." She looked at her hands clasped tightly together in her lap, then lifted her head and met his eyes directly.

"You knew that you were adopted?"

Again the blue eyes narrowed as they studied her. There was an almost imperceptible lowering of his clefted chin to indicate an affirmative answer.

She drew a deep breath. "I've been looking for you for years, Kenneth. I'm your sister."

His face registered no expression. She sat tensely, waiting for some reaction. Erin had expected him to rush across the rug and embrace her, laugh, cry, curse, show dismay, anything but sit there and stare at her with his masklike face fixed in rigid lines.

Finally, he reached for the eyeglasses on top of his head and took them off, twirling the stem in his hand as he said, "My sister?"

"Yes!" She nodded her head enthusiastically, making her short dark curls bounce. "I know it's incredible, but it's true! May I tell you what I know?"

"Please." He still wasn't excited about her revelation, but at least he was responding. More than anything she wanted to dispel his wariness of her.

"We were adopted from a small Catholic orphanage in Los Angeles. Did you know that?"

"I think so," he answered noncommittally.

"You are three years older than I. Our mother gave us up for adoption when I was only several months old. I was adopted by a couple named O'Shea. Soon after they got me, they moved to Houston, Texas, where I grew up. It wasn't until I was in high school that I began to be bothered about who I was and where I came from. I guess that's true of all adolescents, but having been adopted, it was even more important for me to find my roots, so to speak. I'm sure you can relate to that feeling."

"Yes," he said. He was slouching in the over-stuffed chair with his arms folded across his chest.

It was a relaxed position, but Erin sensed that his insouciance was deceptive. Her brother seemed never to be totally relaxed.

"It was years later that I was finally able, financially and every other way, to begin an earnest search for my true identity. There are organizations now that help adopted children locate their natural parents or lost siblings. Believe me, by now I know them all. I left no stone unturned. Almost four years ago—"

She broke off when the red telephone on the desk rang. With the alacrity of a striking snake, he uncoiled himself from the chair and shot across the room. He jerked up the instrument in the middle of its second ring and answered with a curt "Yes." He listened for a moment, never diverting his eyes from Erin's astonished face. "Yeah. No, everything's cool. I'll be in touch." He replaced the telephone receiver and then returned to his chair. "Go on," he said calmly.

Erin was nonplussed by his abrupt, economical movements. Didn't one usually say "Excuse me" when they answered the telephone while engaged in conversation with someone else? And why had he *attacked* the telephone instead of answering it casually? Was he expecting an important call?

"Well, I . . ." she stammered. What had she been saying? He seemed suspicious of her losing her train of thought.

"You were saying, 'Almost four years ago . . .' "

"Oh, yes," she said nervously. "Almost four

years ago, I began an extensive search for our natural parents. My adoptive mother understood this compulsion I had to find them and supplied me with the name of the orphanage in Los Angeles. I was heartsick to discover that sometime subsequent to our being adopted, it had burned and all the records with it. That set me back for months. Finally, I was able to locate a nun who had been at the orphanage at the time we were brought in. That was when I first learned about you.'' To her chagrin, her voice began to quiver and she could feel tears filling her dark, liquid eyes.

"Can you understand my happiness that day? I had a brother! Someone I shared a heritage with. I began to examine faces in a crowd. Each man of your age, I studied, wondering if he might be you. I won't bore you with all the tedious details now, but I traced your adoptive parents. That was relatively simple since they had stayed in Los Angeles. I'm sorry about their demise. They were killed several years ago, I believe?''

"Yes.''

"I lost Dad, Mr. O'Shea, when I was in college. I hope you were as lucky as I with the family who adopted you. The O'Sheas loved me as if I were their own flesh and blood. And I love them.''

"Yes, my parents, or rather, the Lymans, were terrific.''

"Oh, I'm so glad,'' she enthused. "One of the agencies I was telling you about helped me trace you here. I know all about you, but not nearly as much as I want to know. I want to know everything about you, your life.''

The glasses were precariously clinging to the tip of his nose, and he stared at her over their frames. Now he took them off and placed them on the table at his elbow. ''That's quite a story,'' he said. ''We don't look much like each other. Who would believe that we're brother and sister?''

She laughed, glad now that they seemed to be sharing a normal conversation. The hard lines around his mouth had softened. She must be patient with him. After all, she had dumped quite a load on him today. ''I thought the same thing when you answered the door. There's no resemblance at all.''

His eyes were taking in each feature of her face and she sat still while he perused her, allowing him the same privilege she had afforded herself when she first saw him.

He scanned the tumbled sable curls that surrounded her head and fanned away from her face. Dark, smooth brows arched winglike over her eyes—Natalie Wood eyes, one of her high school sweethearts had dubbed them. They were round and large and as dark as ebony. When she lived in New York, she had consulted a makeup expert who taught her how to accent them with just the right touch of pencils and shadows. The result was heart-stopping to someone meeting her for the first time. Her eyes expressed more of what Erin felt and thought than words ever could.

It made her nervous for her brother to examine her

with such keen interest. His eyes dwelt an inordinate amount of time on her lips which were soft and moist and accustomed to smiling.

As his eyes traveled from her chin down her throat, he seemed to take note that her smooth complexion, delicately fair in contrast to her dark hair and eyes, extended to her neck and beyond.

Erin smoothed imaginary wrinkles from the skirt of her white wool suit as he continued to appraise her. The emerald green silk blouse she wore under her jacket suddenly seemed stifling, especially when his eyes lingered on the single strand of coral beads that rested on her breasts. She uncrossed her legs self-consciously when his eyes raked them from her knees to the toes of her brown suede pumps.

His eyes returned to her face and he stood up, crossing the room to stand in front of her. "Not every man is fortunate enough to have a sister," he said quietly as he looked down at her. "Learning of her existence in midlife is a phenomenon. Having her be as lovely as you is a rare pleasure indeed."

She blushed happily. "Thank you, Kenneth." He was proud of her! Perhaps in time she and this stranger could come to know and like each other— maybe even grow to love each other.

"Would you like something to drink?" He held out his hand and she accepted it unhesitantly as he helped her off the cushions of the couch. His hand was warm as he clasped her fingers fleetingly.

"Yes, thank you. The flight was crowded and I was too excited and in too big a hurry to stop for anything before coming here. I hope you don't think it was rude of me to just drop in like this. I thought it best to meet you in person and not try to introduce myself over the telephone.''

"You were right. I'm glad you came straight here.''

He was propelling her through the house—down the main hallway, through a dining room—into a sunny kitchen. She looked at the view out the window. Kenneth's house was situated on a hill, but unfortunately it didn't provide a view of the bay, or the Golden Gate Bridge, or any other distinctive landmark of this fabulous city. Instead, the view was dotted with the rooftops of houses on the lower slopes of the hillside.

Kenneth offered her a chair at the small round table that stood in the center of the kitchen. "What will you have? Coke? Beer? Wine?''

"Coke, please,'' she said. "I'm anxious to meet your wife. Does she know that you were adopted?''

He ignored her question as he opened a can of the soft drink and reached for two glasses in the cabinet over the counter top. As he chunked ice cubes into the glasses he said, "Melanie should be back shortly. She went out to run a few errands.''

"How long have you been married?''

He paused as he handed her the glass of Coke. "Several years now,'' he answered lightly. He smiled charmingly, and for the first time Erin saw two rows of perfectly matched, startling white teeth. He really was quite handsome when he wasn't wearing that surly, suspicious expression. "You're married, I see," he commented nonchalantly as he took the chair across the table from hers.

She followed the direction of his eyes to the large diamond ring on her left ring finger. "No," she muttered. "Just engaged." For some reason, she didn't want to tell him about Bart right now. Bart had a way of dominating a conversation, and she didn't want even a mention of him to intrude on the special, rare intimacy of this first meeting with her brother. "Tell me about your work," she blurted out in order to change the subject.

"What about it?" he asked evenly. Erin was alarmed to see that he was staring at her again with that narrow-eyed stare that made her feel like a laboratory animal under a glass.

"What exactly do you do? I know you work at a bank."

"Yeah," he shrugged. "I guess I do a little of everything."

"I see," she said, though she didn't.

"You?" he asked. "What do you do?"

"I have my own business in Houston."

The thick golden eyebrows raised in silent query. "What kind of business?" He leaned his elbows on the table and propped his chin on his fists. The backs of his hands and his knuckles were sprinkled with crinkly blond hairs. His fingers were long and tapering, not thick and stubby like Bart's. His nails were well cared for, she noted objectively.

Erin raised her eyes to his. She could barely see

the blue irises through the brush of thick eyelashes that screened them. His good looks made her uneasy. It was almost as if his handsomeness were a barrier to her getting to know him better. For some reason intimacy between them seemed dangerous.

"I . . . uh . . . my business organizes and stages fashion shows," she answered.

"I've never heard of anything like that," he said.

She laughed. "That's what makes us unique!" she piped and playfully tapped his hand with her own.

Exhibiting that same swiftness of action she had witnessed before, he captured her hand with his and held it tightly. For endless moments they stared across the table at each other. When he spoke, it was in a low, vibrating voice.

"You said a few minutes ago that you wanted to get to know me. I want to know you, too. I think we should start now, don't you?"

She swallowed convulsively and wished he would release her hand. It would be useless to try to retrieve it. His fingers seemed to be made of steel. She could see herself reflected in the pupils of his eyes, and her own revealing expression frightened her. She whispered tremulously, "Start what?"

"Start getting to know each other."

Before she could blink, he had stood up and come around the table. Before she could breathe, he had pulled her to her feet and encircled her with his arms. One hand embedded itself in her dark, rich curls as he tilted her head back and looked down into her face.

"What better way to get to know each other than with a kiss of reciprocal filial affection?"

The face that descended toward hers bespoke nothing of brotherly fondness. That was Erin's last conscious thought before she felt his mouth invade hers. His fingers were wound so tightly through her hair that tears of pain joined those of mortification that had already flooded her eyes. His other arm was secure across the middle of her back, pinning her arms to her sides and pressing her against his unyielding body.

She squirmed against him, but her movements only strengthened his hold on her. Deep in her throat she screamed, screams that were swallowed by his mouth that covered and absorbed hers. Her lips throbbed under the bruising pressure of his, and they were powerless to prevent his relentless tongue from entering her mouth.

Never had she been kissed like this. It was disgusting. It was a heinous sin. Knowing their relationship, the way he explored her mouth was decadent and revolting.

It was also thrilling.

She struggled for control—not physical control. Her limbs had been rendered useless and, to her shame, she leaned into him for support. She was fighting a losing struggle of the will.

She fought the sensations that danced up and down her spine. They were responsible for the trembling, melting warmth in the pit of her stomach that she strove to ignore. Her eyes, which had been opened wide with surprise and indignation, now closed of their own volition, disobeying her cerebral commands to remain open and scorn this odious man.

The rattle of a key being inserted in the back door lock saved Erin from the absolute degradation of submission. She renewed her struggling until she managed to push away from him, when he raised his head and relaxed his arms. He faced the door, though he kept a firm grip on Erin's upper arm.

The woman who came through the door was dainty, young, and blond. She was smiling in a childlike manner despite the sadness that clouded her brown eyes and attested to some deep worry.

The two people standing in the middle of the room were frozen in a caricature of an embrace. The woman's expression was bleak and guilty, her features ravaged, her face pale.

The man's mien was hard, cold, and fearsome. It was toward him that the blond woman turned quizzical eyes.

"Hello, Mrs. Lyman."

"Mr. Barrett," she answered shyly. "Wha—"

"Mrs. Lyman, do you know this woman?" he interrupted her. "Have you ever seen her before?"

The young woman addressed as Mrs. Lyman by a man who was supposed to be her husband looked at Erin and shook her head. "No, Mr. Barrett, I've never seen her before."

Barrett! Barrett!

Erin raised incredulous eyes to the man who still retained a steel-band grip on her arm. The blue eyes that met hers were frigid and implacable.

"Who are you?" she demanded.

CHAPTER
Two

"That's what I was about to ask you, lady," he snarled as he cruelly ushered her across the kitchen. He called to the stunned Melanie Lyman over his shoulder, "Mrs. Lyman, please call across the street and ask Mike to come over here and monitor the telephone. Tell him to run a check on the car outside. I'll be in the study, but I'd rather not be disturbed unless it's urgent. And please don't go out unless you take one of the boys with you."

"No, I won't," Erin heard her say meekly. Apparently she was accustomed to taking orders from this brute, but Erin O'Shea was not. As soon as she could she was going to bring down such wrath on him that he wouldn't know what had hit him.

He pushed her into a small paneled room and slammed the door behind them, latching it soundly. She whirled around to face him, ready to do battle. To her horror, he roughly pulled her jacket from her

shoulders and down her arms. He tossed it across
the room where it plopped onto a leather sofa. She
was too astounded to protest when he yanked the
bottom of her blouse out of the skirt's waistband.
He shoved her against the nearest wall, turned her
around to face it, and raised her hands wide over
her head.

She gasped in humiliation and repulsion when he
clamped his hands under her arms and slid them
down her sides. Inexorably, they moved around her
rib cage, over her breasts, between them, and down
to her waist. They insinuated themselves into the
waistband of her skirt where they explored her abdomen and hips. When they had toured down the outside of her thighs, he swung her around to face him.

She never remembered being as furious as she
was at that moment. Her blood boiled in her veins,
making the pulse in her head pound. Erin blinked
to clear her vision, which was impaired by rage.

"Aren't you going to strip search me?" she
sneered.

"Only if I think it's necessary. Which at the
present, I don't. But don't press your luck."

His smug answer infuriated her further and she
struggled to push him away from her and put more
space between them. Surprisingly he obliged her
and took a step backward.

"Who the hell do you think you are to treat me
this way? I demand an explanation from you this
instant!" She knew her words would carry little
weight with this bully. They sounded trite and melo-

dramatic and childish to her own ears, but her brain was whirling, and she didn't seem capable of being more eloquent.

"Easy, lady. I'm about to identify myself to you and then we'll cut all this temper tantrum crap and get down to finding out who you are—which is more to the point."

He took a wallet out of his hip pocket and flipped it open. He held it inches in front of her eyes so that she could read: Lawrence James Barrett, United States Department of the Treasury.

Her wide eyes flew from the official badge to his eyes, which bored into her. She could actually feel herself melting under that hard gaze. Energy and anger seeped out of her.

God! What had she stumbled into?

"Pleased to meet you, Miss O'Shea," he said sarcastically. Taking her arm no less firmly than he had before, he pushed her toward the leather couch. "Sit down and don't move," he commanded.

Erin was too stunned and bewildered to object, and instinctively she obeyed him and sank down onto the sofa. Mr. Barrett picked up her jacket and searched the pockets. Finding nothing, he dropped it back on the sofa. Absently Erin folded it and placed it beside her. She didn't feel like putting it back on or tucking in her blouse. A fever seemed to have washed over her, and her skin was prickly with abnormal heat.

He went to the door and opened it. "Mike?" he shouted.

"Yeah, Lance."

"Bring me that purse on the sofa in the living room, please."

"Sure thing," the anonymous voice answered back.

"And see if you can locate my glasses."

"They're on the table next to the chair you sat in," Erin answered automatically. He swiveled his head toward her in surprise. She could have bitten her tongue. Now he knew she had noticed him and his subconscious mannerisms.

"Check the end table," he said through the door.

While he waited for his subordinate to carry out his request, Lance Barrett watched Erin. Uncomfortably, she shifted under his stare and again felt like a specimen that required careful observation. She tried to meet his stare boldly and knew that she failed miserably. In her life, she had never felt more nervous or astonished at a turn of events. To borrow an expression from her mother, she was flabbergasted.

Mike was a younger man than his superior, short, with black hair. His features were nondescript. He had been chosen well for this type of work, Erin thought to herself. No one would ever remember him. He would remain faceless in a crowd.

Mr. Barrett took his glasses and her purse from the younger man and asked, "The car?"

Mike glanced at Erin, but his face registered no expression. Another characteristic of his trade, she thought. "Clean, Lance. It was leased just after noon today at San Francisco International."

"Okay, thanks." Mike turned to go, but Mr. Barrett halted him. "Bring me everything in the car—bags, luggage, anything else you see that might be important. It's still unlocked?"

Mike nodded and left, closing the door behind him.

Mr. Barrett faced her and treated her again to one of his long, uncompromising stares. Putting the glasses on, he said, "All right, Miss O'Shea, start talking." He sauntered over to a game table and unceremoniously dumped the contents of her purse onto its green felt surface.

"I'm not saying a thing until you tell me what this is about. By what license do you insult me and question me like this? What has happened? And, Mr. Barrett, I intend to complain to your superiors about your uncouth and unnecessarily rough treatment."

He quirked one of the golden eyebrows at her and seemed faintly amused by her show of bravado. "Go ahead. Complain. We're accused of much worse every day. It's my word against yours. Anyway, lady, you aren't exactly in a position to start issuing ultimatums. Any minute now, I may get mad as hell at you. Believe me, that's something you'd be wise to avoid." His eyes raked her insolently and she blushed when she remembered how he had kissed her. Why had he done that?

"Start talking," he warned in a low, sinister voice.

All right, Mr. Government Agent, I'll play your little game for a while and you'll suffer later for humiliating me this way. "What do you want to know?" she asked tartly.

"Your name."

"I've already told you."

"Tell me again."

She sighed. "Erin O'Shea."

"Address."

"4435 Meadowbrook Road, Houston, Texas."

"That's what it says on the driver's license. Very good," he said. All the while she was talking, he had been rifling through the items in her purse. He had studied her driver's license, thumbed through the money in her wallet, looked through her checkbook, and scanned the list of stubbed checks. "Go on," he said.

"What—"

"What are you doing here?"

"I told you that, too," she said crossly. Her patience with this creep had just about played out. She was quickly tiring of his game of cops and robbers.

He looked up at her with dark, hooded eyes and said, "Tell me again." His cold, steely voice brooked no argument.

"I was adopted when I was an infant. For several years I have been looking for my natural parents and a brother whom I discovered I had. We were separated when we were adopted by different families. Apparently the agencies weren't sensitive about things like that then."

He had unzipped her clear plastic makeup bag and was inspecting each lipstick, compact, and small container for its contents. He sniffed appreciatively at a cut glass travel atomizer of Lauren perfume. He opened a pillbox and took out a small white tablet.

"That's aspirin," she said defensively.

He nodded and recapped the box. "I haven't made any accusations," he countered. "Go on."

"I learned that Kenneth Lyman is my brother. I came here today from Houston to introduce myself to him. That's all there is. You know the rest. Please tell me what all of this is about."

He rezipped the cosmetic bag and tossed it onto the table. After pushing the glasses to the top of his head, he hitched one hip over the corner of the table and folded his arms across his chest. Watching her closely, he said, "Kenneth Lyman embezzled seven hundred and fifty thousand dollars from the Yerba Buena National Bank ten days ago. He hasn't been seen or heard from since."

The level, distinct words hit Erin like a cannonball in the chest. Their impact was forceful. For several moments, she couldn't breathe, and when she did, it was in quick, insufficient pants.

Before she could form any response to this devastating piece of news, Mike opened the door and carried in her two pieces of luggage and her leather

trench coat. He deposited the suitcases on the floor
and draped the coat over a chair. Then he left as
unobtrusively as he had come.

"Let's try again, Miss O'Shea, if indeed that is
your name," Mr. Barrett said. "How long have you
known Lyman?"

Erin turned wide, disbelieving eyes on him. "I
. . . I've never met him," she gasped. "I told you
that I—"

"I know what you told me, Miss O'Shea. But
you'll have to admit it's a pretty farfetched story.
Come on and level with me. Were you in on this
job with Lyman?"

"What!" She jumped off the couch. "You must
be crazy!"

"Sit down," he growled ominously. She retreated from that terrible, threatening face until the
backs of her knees touched the sofa and she collapsed on it. "I have never met my brother," she
declared slowly.

He knelt on the floor beside her luggage and un-
snapped the latch. Frilly underwear and nightgowns
spilled over his hands as he spread the hinged halves
apart. Lifting each garment, he gave it a thorough
inspection.

One sheer blue nightgown with an ecru lace bodice caught his attention. Slowly, he drew it across
his palm. Looking up at her he said, "Very nice."
Erin flushed hotly with embarrassment and anger.
"I'm waiting," he said, as he continued to examine
the articles in her suitcase.

"For what? A confession?" she asked sweetly.

He was up off the floor and leaning over her before the last word was out of her mouth. "Dammit, I'm getting weary of your sly, glib answers. I want the truth from you and I want it now. Do you understand me?" He had placed his hands on either side of her hips, imprisoning her beneath him. She felt his breath, hot and insistent, on her face. His eyes were incredibly blue and struck her with sparks of anger.

"Yes," she ground out through clenched teeth.

Gradually he straightened up and backed away from her. Was he disappointed with himself for momentarily losing control? It seemed to take an effort to restore himself to the cool, impersonal government agent.

"What kind of business are you in?"

"I've already told . . ." She broke off immediately when she saw his beginning scowl. She swallowed her proud anger and answered. "The name of my company is Spotlight. We organize fashion shows for department stores, organizations, individuals, whoever needs our services. We do everything from hiring models and selecting the featured clothes to ordering the flowers and refreshments."

"Forgive me, Miss O'Shea, but no average working girl rents a Mercedes, carries five hundred and sixty dollars in cash in her purse, and wears Oscar de la Renta suits."

How had he been able to count those bills he had casually thumbed through? How had he known whose label was in her suit? She glanced down at the jacket lying beside her on the sofa and saw that the label was readily apparent for someone who had the eyes of an eagle and the cunning of a fox.

He saw her puzzling this out and said, "I may be an 'uncouth' G-man, but I *have* heard of Oscar de la Renta, and I know that suit you're wearing must have set you back what I make in a week. Where do you get money like that, Miss O'Shea?"

"I earn it," she shouted. "I'm not an 'average working girl,' Mr. Barrett. I own my company and have an office staff of twelve talented people. My business is an extremely successful one."

"Congratulations," he sneered. "How did you get the capital to start a business like that?"

"From my husband."

Her answer seemed to take him by surprise and his eyes narrowed on her menacingly. "You told me earlier that you weren't married."

"I'm not," she said. When she saw him take a step toward her, she held up both hands, palms out. "I'm a widow."

His reaction to that statement was totally unexpected. He threw back his head and bellowed with laughter. "Oh boy. You don't miss a trick, do you? I can't wait to hear this tale," he said with a chuckle.

"It's true!" she cried.

"Please continue. I'm breathless with anticipation." He gave her a mocking bow.

"As soon as I graduated from college, I went to New York. I worked there for two years as a model.

I wasn't very successful as a glamour model, so I went to work in one of the apparel manufacturing firms as a house model.''

She could tell by his skeptical expression that she wasn't explaining too well. "You see, each line, each fashion house, has a model by which to gauge their sizes. I had the measurements of a perfect size eight. They made all their patterns by adjusting them to my figure—as long as I maintained the correct measurements.''

She licked her lips nervously, for he was assessing her figure as if trying to decide if she had perfect measurements or not. "It—it was a good job because when I wasn't needed by the designers or seamstresses, I learned about the business—design, color, fabric, accessories, even shipping and billing.''

"I thought all models were tall, skinny, and flat-chested. You, Miss O'Shea," he grinned slyly, "are tall, *slender*, but definitely not flat-chested.''

Erin's cheeks were suffused with hot color and her only response was a mumbled, "I told you I wasn't a successful glamour model.''

After a long, uncomfortable silence, he asked, "What happened to this fairy tale job?''

"I got married.''

"Oh, yes, I had almost forgotten the husband.''

Erin bit back an angry retort and said levelly, "The owner of the company married me. We had been married only a few months when the doctors diagnosed terminal cancer. He died. He left me some money. I moved back to Houston and established Spotlight."

"He was older than you?"

"Considerably."

"So you live off this inheritance and rent a Mercedes with it?"

"No, Mr. Barrett. I do not," she stated heatedly. "He had two grown children from his first marriage. The bulk of his estate went to them. I asked that he leave me with only enough money to get my business established."

"How generous of you." He was now going through the contents of her smaller suitcase. The articles were distinctly feminine and she resented this invasion of privacy. She would have no secrets from this loathsome man.

He held up a package of tablets and raised an eyebrow in query. "Birth control pills?"

She was seething over his audacity. "No. An antibiotic. I had a sore throat last week."

"This isn't how a prescription is usually packaged."

"I got it at the doctor's office from his sample drug supply. He saved me a trip to the pharmacy."

He seemed satisfied with her answer. While he was sniffing at a bar of perfumed soap he said, "You must truly think I'm stupid, Miss O'Shea. You go by your maiden name, right?" She nodded. "Why? Are you ashamed of marrying some old man with cancer and inheriting his money when he conveniently croaked?"

She felt the blood draining from her head only to return to it in a rushing flood. Catapulting off the sofa, she flew across the floor toward him and raised her hand intending to deliver a well-deserved, resounding slap to his self-satisfied face. Her hand was caught in midair and her arm was twisted behind her back painfully.

He drew her against him, holding her defenseless and immobile. "I wouldn't ever try that again if I were you," he threatened convincingly. "Now, why don't you use your married name? If there is such a thing."

"My married name was Greene. I was married to Joseph Greene. His name is well-known in the garment industry even now. I don't use his name because sanctimonious, chauvinistic bastards like you might think that it was his name and money and not hours of hard work that made my business a success."

His arms tightened around her and she gasped in pain from the way he bent her arm behind her. She met his cold blue stare with one of her own.

Crowding her anger was a sudden confusion. The ache in her arm was nothing compared with the painful awareness of his body conforming to hers. The chest that crushed her breasts felt like a brick wall. Hard thighs moved against hers until they found a position that was an agreeable fit.

The cold blue light in his eyes that moments ago had flared angrily, began to burn with something that was much more fearsome. Each feature of her face came under hot blue flame and she felt like her eyes, temples, cheeks, and lips were being licked with tongues of fire.

Acknowledging, but unable to tolerate, the squeezing pleasure in her chest, Erin lowered her eyes. Immediately she felt that leashed tension in the body next to hers abating, and he released her.

She turned her back, composed her features, and, because there was nothing else to do, resumed her seat on the leather sofa.

"Who's the boyfriend?" he asked, indicating the enormous ring on her left hand. Did his voice sound different? Less assured? A trifle shaky?

"My fiancé's name is Bart Stanton. He's a Houston businessman."

He guffawed again with sardonic laughter. "Bart Stanton! Bart, for God's sake," he said, chuckling. "Does he drive an El Dorado with a pair of longhorns mounted on the hood?"

"I don't have to take any more of your insults, Mr. Barrett!"

"You'll take anything I damn well please," he exploded, all mirth gone. "I don't believe for one minute that you're who or what you say you are. I think that you were some kind of contact for Lyman. You showed up today expecting him and got me instead. You spun this tall tale and hoped that I'd be stupid enough to fall for it. Guess again, lady."

"Will you please stop calling me lady. You know my name."

"At least the one you gave me, Miss O'Shea. Or is it Ms.? Never mind," he said when he saw her about to protest. "Now that I think of it, O'Shea is an Irish name. And you said you were adopted from a Catholic orphanage. Was the seven hundred and fifty thousand dollars by any chance going to be used to purchase weapons to be shipped to northern Ireland? Or maybe you were here to sell drugs. Or buy drugs. I don't know yet, but I'll find out."

"You are mad," she whispered hoarsely. "All you have to do is check my credentials. Call my business. Call Bart."

"You don't sound like a Texan."

"I lived in New York for five years. I lost my accent."

"If what you say is true, who knew that you were on this fantastic search for your long lost brother?"

"The people I work with. Bart. My mother, Mrs. Merle O'Shea. She lives in Shreveport, Louisiana."

He was taking notes on a pad he had taken out of his shirt pocket. He paused in his scribbling. "You said she lived in Houston."

"She moved to Louisiana to live with her sister when my father, Gerald O'Shea, died."

"What's the sister's name?" he asked brusquely. Erin supplied it. "Phone number." She gave him her aunt's telephone number and address.

He flipped the cardboard binding over the notes he had just taken and said, "Make yourself comfortable, Miss O'Shea. I've got some phone calls to make.'' He went to the door and turned back to her with his hand on the knob. ''Incidentally, Mike will be just outside the door.''

''Do you expect me to pull a machine gun from under my skirt and blow this joint?'' she asked with all the venom she could muster.

''No, I don't,'' he drawled. ''I know what's under your skirt.'' His eyes toured her body insultingly before he stepped into the hall and closed the door behind him.

Erin fumed, paced, ranted, cried, and cursed Mr. Lawrence Barrett for the next half hour. When none of those energy-draining pursuits produced results or altered her situation, she resignedly knelt down on the floor and restored some order to her suitcases. Her hand trembled when she touched the nightgown he had handled with what could only be considered a caress.

He was a horrible man, issuing orders, bullying everyone, insulting her for no just cause. Each of his actions had been brutal, even when he had kissed her. Why did her mind persist in dwelling on that when she wanted to push any recollections of the incident into the further recesses of her mind?

She consoled herself on one thing: he wasn't her brother; incest wasn't among his sins.

I won't think about that kiss, she averred to herself. Nor would she think about that unfamiliar fluttering in her stomach each time Mr. Barrett fixed her with that penetrating stare of his. It had been strictly an involuntary reaction when her lips had parted slightly as his eyes devoured them while he held her close. Erin O'Shea had had nothing to do with that. Positively.

Then why was she arguing with herself?

Her head was resting against the back of the sofa and her eyes were closed when he opened the door. She jumped in startled reaction. Had she drifted off to sleep?

"Luck just isn't with you today, Miss O'Shea."

"What do you mean?" She was angry to find that her voice was quivering with apprehension.

"I got a listing for Spotlight from long distance directory assistance. No answer."

"What?" she cried. Then she realized the reason. She checked her gold wristwatch. "It's after six o'clock in Houston. Everyone's gone home," she wailed.

"Bart Stanton has gone to the Panhandle for the next two days. There is no answer at the number in Shreveport."

She rubbed her brow with anxious fingers. *Think, Erin,* she commanded herself. But her brain was spinning with the events of the past few hours. It seemed eons ago since she had stepped onto the airplane in Houston this morning. She was exhausted and couldn't think clearly. Too many unpredictable, inconceivable events had bombarded her in the space of one afternoon.

"One thing I did learn that's in your favor. I asked Mrs. Lyman if her husband was adopted. He was."

"Then surely you believe me." She hated the pleading sound in her voice and the tears that she could feel welling up in the corners of her ebony eyes.

"I'm getting closer," he admitted.

"Oh, thank you, Mr. Barrett. If you don't mind, I'll go now. It has been a long, tiring day to say the least. I'll be at the Fairmont if you need to ask me any more questions. Naturally, I'm upset about my brother and will want to know what happens. I won't leave San Francisco until this whole mess is cleared up."

She picked up her purse and jacket and the leather coat and headed for the door. She never reached it. Mr. Barrett put a restraining hand on her shoulder and took her purse out of her hand.

"Wrong again, Miss O'Shea. You're not going anywhere. You're spending the night here. With me."

CHAPTER

Three

It was with blank, uncomprehending eyes that Erin turned toward the man who had forcefully prevented her from leaving the room. His face was unreadable, but stern.

When the message of his words finally pierced the muddled confusion of her brain, Erin yanked her shoulder from under his hand and retreated several steps.

"You have surely lost your mind, Mr. Barrett."

"I'd concede that if I were to let you leave this house without knowing exactly who you are and why you showed up on Lyman's doorstep this afternoon."

He turned away from her in dismissal and went to the door. Facing her again he said, "As it is, I'm quite sane." He smiled a charming, friendly smile that made her tremble with fury. "You'll excuse me, please. I have work to do. Make yourself comfortable. You have the run of this room.''

"Go to hell," she hissed.

His smile only deepened. "More than likely I will."

He was two steps beyond the door when she flung it open. With a deadly accurate precision, he whirled around and confronted her.

"You can't keep me here like a prisoner!" she shouted.

"No? Who's going to stop me?" he challenged, relaxing somewhat now that he saw she posed no real threat.

She opened her mouth to offer a scathing reply, but no words came out. Who indeed would stop him? Unconsciously her shoulders slumped as she sighed heavily. Why was she fighting an immovable object? She could endure anything for one night. In the morning, he would call Houston, have her identity confirmed, her purpose for seeking out Kenneth Lyman explained to his satisfaction, and then she would never have to see this man again.

Lance Barrett watched Erin closely and could almost read the thoughts as they paraded across her mind. It was his job to discern what people were truly thinking, feeling, despite what they said, and he had been trained well.

Damn! She is a beautiful woman, he thought. When he had opened that door and seen her standing on the porch looking like something out of a fashion magazine, he felt as though he had been slugged in the belly by an iron fist. Of course, that initial impact had soon been put down and his professional caution had taken over. Still, he couldn't take his eyes off her.

There was more to her than a beautiful, sexy package, though. She had gumption and brains. This was no cringing, cowering female whom he could usually reduce to jelly with one of his accusing stares. Erin O'Shea had defied him repeatedly. Hell, he had almost enjoyed their sparring.

He shouldn't have kissed her. He'd get his ass kicked all the way back to Washington if anybody found out about that. And she was right. The way he had searched her had been unnecessary. *Admit it, buddy, you just wanted to get your hands on her.*

Hell, all a man had to do was look at her and he could see every curve and hollow of her compact body under that well-tailored, perfectly fitting suit. Dammit! It *had* cost more than he made in a week and that galled him.

He watched her now as she gnawed on her full bottom lip with small, straight, white teeth. The emotions played across her face like a graphic motion picture. She wasn't any crook and he knew it. That story she had told him had been too fantastic to have been fabricated. If the truth were known, he could easily let her leave and send one of the boys out to keep an eye on her.

Then why didn't he?

Lance had been trained to keep his face immobile and inscrutable. Therefore, Erin didn't see any evidence of his thought pattern concerning her as she looked up at him. She decided to make the best of this horrendous situation.

"It seems I have no choice, Mr. Barrett. I'll stay here until morning when I expect you to make whatever telephone calls are necessary to prove to yourself that what I've told you is the truth."

"Your patriotic cooperation is commendable," he taunted.

She stymied the compulsion to slap his confident, sardonic face and asked, "May I visit with Melanie? We haven't even been properly introduced and she is my sister-in-law. This must be a dreadful time for her."

"I don't see any harm in that. I'll send her in to you. For the time being, I'd rather you stay in this room."

"I promise not to make a run for it."

"Good." He walked away from her.

So much for an attempt at humor, Erin thought dryly as she returned to the paneled room. The man wasn't human. Ice water had replaced the blood in his veins. He must see every Clint Eastwood movie and pattern himself after the hard-nosed, super-macho man.

She had to give him credit for being thorough in his job. He was, after all, a government official with a very difficult chore to do. He must have had years of disciplined training. Now she understood why his eyes never seemed to miss anything. From the time he had opened the front door to her, she felt as though he had seen each movement she had made and read each thought.

She went toward the window and gazed out. She swallowed tightly. Hopefully, he hadn't read all her thoughts. Some of them regarding him she would rather keep private.

Her heart had lurched when he informed her that she would be spending the night with him. Of course, that was only a figure of speech. That wasn't what he *meant*. It had only *sounded* like that's what he meant. Still, it would be costly to her self-esteem if he knew how drastically his choice of words had affected her.

A rosy blush stained her cheeks as she remembered that deep, breathless kiss in the kitchen. Her palms moved up to cup her hot cheeks when she recalled the way she had begun to respond to it before Melanie Lyman had fortunately interrupted. Even when she thought he was her brother, she had almost been guilty of returning his kiss. Had she ever been so instantaneously attracted to a man? Any man?

She looked down at the sparkling diamond mounted on the wide gold band around her finger and smiled ruefully. Bart wouldn't appreciate her comparison of his kisses to Lance Barrett's. The score would tilt in the latter's favor.

Erin knew she was being unfair to Bart. Six months ago when he urged her to accept his engagement ring she had done so in order to silence his constant badgerings.

"Come on, honey. Wear it."

"But, Bart—"

"I know, I know, sugar. You're still hesitant to marry again. I promise not to pressure you for a wedding date, if only you'll wear this engagement ring. Besides, if I take it back to the jewelers, it'll be all over Houston tomorrow that Bart Stanton has been jilted." He hung his large head in feigned supplication. As usual, she crumpled under his foolishness.

Laughing, she shoved his massive shoulder. "Oh, please. Spare me the theatrics. Thousands of women would stand in line for weeks, months, for the chance to wear an engagement ring from the legendary Bart Stanton."

"But I only want one woman, sugar." His voice had dropped the teasing banter, and he was serious. Erin knew he was. That was the complicating factor.

They had dated for over a year. Bart was a powerful man in Houston, always keeping in the background, but brandishing a sharp sword in the business community. Few big business deals were made that Bart didn't know about or participate in.

He was a favorite with newspaper and television reporters. He charmed them with his golly-gee, country boy, shy image. But beneath that head of curly dark hair operated a shrewd brain that could con a victim and wring him out before he realized that he had been had.

Being squired by Bart Stanton was no small victory, and Erin was envied for that rare privilege.

When with him, she was treated like royalty, and it had been fun. But then she began to notice that Bart's feelings were moving toward something stronger than affection, and she couldn't reciprocate it. As much as she liked him, respected him for his business acumen, and enjoyed his company, she didn't love him.

"I'll wear the ring, Bart. But please understand that it's not a binding commitment. I still don't want to marry anytime soon. And this doesn't mean that I'll change my mind about . . . about . . ."

"Sleeping with me?" he asked in as soft a voice as Bart could manage.

She met his dark eyes levelly. "Yes."

"Damned if you aren't the stubbornest woman I've ever met," he said with agitation. Then he chuckled. "Maybe that's why I love you so much, baby." He had enfolded her in a crushing embrace, and they had sealed their engagement with a kiss.

Oddly, he hadn't asked her to sleep with him since. Until then, it had been a constant source of tension between them.

"It's not as if you're a virgin or something," he had railed at her the first time she had refused his practiced invitation for her to stay the night at his sprawling Houston home. "You've been married, for God's sake."

She had been adamant then and continued to be. Apparently, since she had accepted the ring that branded her as his possession, he had found an outlet for his sexual frustration. Perversely, Erin was grateful to that anonymous woman—or women—who was supplying Bart with something she couldn't give him.

The late afternoon San Francisco sun made rainbows on the facets of the diamond as she turned it on her finger. She sighed in resolution. As soon as she returned to Houston she would have to level with Bart. She had used the excuse of finding her brother for long enough. He would be expecting to proceed with wedding plans. If she had ever wavered in her decision before, after experiencing Lance Barrett's kiss, Erin knew now for a certainty that she would never marry Bart Stanton.

Her reverie was interrupted when the door to the room opened, and she turned to see Melanie's blond head peering around it.

"Miss O'Shea?" she asked timidly. "Mr. Barrett said you wanted to see me."

Erin suppressed the strong urge to laugh. She was in this woman's house, and yet the hostess was almost asking Erin's permission to enter the room.

She crossed the room quickly and extended both hands to her sister-in-law. "Melanie."

The young woman closed the door behind her and took both of Erin's hands. They stared at each other for long moments, taking their measure of each other, and then it seemed the most natural thing in the world to come together in a sisterly embrace.

Erin's heart constricted when she felt sobs wracking Melanie's slender frame. Erin didn't mind the tears that would stain her silk shirt as they fell on her shoulders. She stroked Melanie's long, straight hair and shushed her, assuring her that everything would be well.

Tears were smarting in her own eyes by the time Melanie's anguish had been spent and she pushed away from Erin. "We're being terribly silly, aren't we?" Erin said. "Let's sit down over here and get better acquainted."

"I'm sorry, Miss O'Shea," Melanie sniffed. "I've needed to do that ever since Ken . . . ever since he . . . did what he did. I can't understand it." She shook her head sadly, staring bleakly into Erin's face.

"Please call me Erin."

"Are you really Ken's sister?" the woman/child asked hopefully.

"As positive as I can be under the circumstances," Erin answered honestly.

"You look like him," Melanie said, looking closely at Erin's face.

"Really?" Erin said with a laugh, delighted at the prospect. "Do you have any pictures of him?"

"Sure. Lots." Melanie bounced off the couch, tears and remorse forgotten temporarily, and opened a drawer in the desk—the desk that Lance Barrett had so negligently leaned against, Erin thought inconsequentially, and hated herself for allowing thoughts of him to enter her mind.

"Here are our wedding pictures," Melanie said.

"How long have you been married?" Hadn't she asked Lance that question? He had given her an evasive answer.

"Four years," Melanie replied as she flopped down beside Erin on the couch and opened a large white padded volume. "Here he is."

Slowly Erin took the photograph album out of Melanie's hands and lifted it toward her. She was unaccountably nervous as she lowered her eyes to the smiling man in the picture.

His image began to blur as her eyes filled with tears and impatiently she wiped them away in order to see him better. He was tall, towering over his bride who looked up at him with worshipful eyes. His hair was as dark as Erin's, though it hadn't been treated to the soft body permanent that hers had, and was combed back straight from his face. The eyes were an unmistakable family trait. His brows arched over his deep ebony eyes exactly as hers did. His mouth was less full, the lips more narrow, but the resemblance between them was striking.

"He's very handsome, isn't he?" Erin asked hoarsely. Her throat was clogged with emotion.

"Yes," agreed Melanie. "I fell in love with him the first time I walked in the bank and saw him behind the teller's counter. I asked Daddy who the new employee was, but he didn't know his name. I made it my business to find out, though!"

"Your father works at the same bank that Ken does?"

"He's the president and chairman of the board,"

Melanie commented absently as she turned the pages of the album.

Erin digested this piece of news as she nodded appreciatively while Melanie pointed out other pictures of Ken. Erin would look at them more closely later in private. Something about Melanie's father being such a top-ranking officer in the bank where her brother was employed bothered her. Would it have bothered Ken as well? Could that be the reason he had embezzled the money?

"Forgive me for being so nosy, Melanie. I want to learn as much about my brother as possible. You're several years younger than he, aren't you?"

"Yes," she admitted, lowering her eyes. "He's ten years older than I am. I was only twenty when we got married. Mother and Daddy had a fit when we announced our plans to them. We had been dating secretly. I think I knew all along that they wouldn't be too happy with me for dating Ken. They wanted me to date the sons of their friends who play tennis and golf at the country club every day and go sailing on the weekends. I just wasn't interested in anybody. I fell in love the first time Ken kissed me and then begged my forgiveness for doing so." Her brown eyes were twinkling when she added, "I assured him, I didn't mind."

But your parents did, thought Erin.

There was a light tap on the door before it opened and Lance walked in. "What would you ladies like for dinner? I thought I'd go out for Chinese food if that's okay with everybody."

Erin couldn't believe his insensitivity. He was treating this bizarre situation like it was a family picnic.

"Chinese food sounds great to me," Melanie said happily. "Do you like it, Erin? If not, we can order something else."

"I thought prisoners were restricted to a diet of bread and water," she said directly to Mr. Barrett.

He glared at her a moment with those cold blue eyes before he growled, "Only the smart-assed ones." The door was shut with emphasis.

"Brute," Erin muttered when he had gone.

"Mr. Barrett?" Melanie asked in an astonished voice. "Why, he's the nicest man I've ever met! Except for Ken, of course."

Erin looked at her in puzzled shock. "You can't be serious! He's practically taken over the control of your house and your life. He issues orders like a drill sergeant and expects everyone to scurry to obey them. He has invaded your privacy to the utmost extreme."

"He's only doing his job, Erin," Melanie said quietly. "Ken is in a lot of trouble, you know. When Mr. Barrett came here, he was apologetic for his intrusion. During the long hours he questioned me, he was a perfect gentleman, and put me at ease when I was frightened and heartsick with worry over Ken and what he had done. He coaxed me into remembering things I never could have otherwise; things that might help them track Ken down. I'll do anything I can to help them. I want them to find Ken and bring him home. I want to know that he's safe."

Erin sympathized with the young woman and even concurred with her hope that Ken Lyman would soon be found. But she was stunned to hear Melanie describing Lance Barrett in such glowing terms. Words like "gentleman," "apologetic," "coax" didn't fit the manner in which the man had treated her.

What made Erin a suspect in crime when he obviously didn't think Ken's wife was in collusion with him? He had abused her physically and verbally since her arrival. What had she done to provoke such harsh treatment?

Melanie insisted that, in spite of everything, Erin's appearance in the house called for a celebration. She cajoled Mike into allowing Erin to leave the study and help her set the dining room table. Using her best tablecloth, china, and crystal, Melanie set the table with the detail required for an important dinner party.

Her attempt was touching and somehow pathetic. She seemed far younger than her twenty-four years. Even though she gave lip service to the seriousness of Ken's theft, Erin doubted that Melanie really grasped it. Naiveté and blind trust were readily apparent in everything she said and did.

The three of them were laughing at a recalcitrant napkin that refused to stand at attention in the china plate as Melanie wanted it to, when Lance came through the door of the dining room.

He wore a scowl of disapproval when he leveled his hard gaze on Erin. Leaving no question of his displeasure at seeing her out of the room where he had sequestered her, he bore down on Mike.

"Uh . . . I . . . she . . . that is, Mrs. Lyman thought . . ." Mike stammered before Lance mercifully cut him off abruptly and said, "Let's eat this before it gets cold."

Mike breathed a visible sigh of relief and cast an eye toward Erin as if blaming her for his transgression. He was quick to hop to Lance's aid in relieving him of some of the cartons of Chinese food. The white pasteboard was incongruous with the fine linen tablecloth and shimmering crystal, but no one seemed to notice as they took their seats around the table.

Erin watched with stunned eyes as Lance helped Melanie into her chair. He was solicitous in manner, and his eyes softened discernibly whenever he looked at her. Erin graciously accepted Mike's help with her own chair. She smiled up at him and said "Thank you," missing the hard, quelling look Mike received from his superior.

Melanie explained to Lance her reason for going to the trouble of using the best dishes and setting the table in the dining room. "It's not every day that one finds out they have a beautiful, sweet sister-in-law. If Ken were here," her voice quivered slightly, "I'm sure that he'd want to celebrate her sudden appearance."

"Did your husband ever mention having a sister that was separated from him?" Lance asked her softly. His tone was deceptive and for Melanie's benefit alone. When he looked at Erin, she shuddered under the glacial stare.

"No. If he knew about Erin, he never told me. He'll be delighted to see her. I know."

"Miss O'Shea." Erin jumped when Lance addressed her. "In this quest for your family, did you make any progress toward finding your parents?"

Coming from someone else, she would have considered that a reasonable question. But she knew that Lance Barrett was only baiting a trap he hoped she'd fall into.

"Unfortunately, no. The nun who told me about Ken remembered only that my mother brought us in together. She didn't remember anything about her or why she . . . why she . . ." As usual when she talked on this subject, her vocal cords tightened, making it difficult for her to add the last words, "abandoned us."

There was a noticeable cessation of dining sounds. No silverware clattered against china, no ice cubes rattled in glasses, no one said a word. Finally Melanie broke the period of suspended animation when she said as sweetly as a child comforting a playmate, "She probably had a very good reason, Erin."

Erin composed her face and looked up at Melanie. Smiling, she said, "Yes, probably."

Conversation during the remainder of the meal was more subdued. Only once did Lance make Melanie laugh when he regaled her with an adventure that he swore was true, but which Erin considered to be highly implausible. He had probably taken a mundane incident and embroidered it to make it seem more intriguing.

Erin conceded him a small amount of her admiration for entertaining Melanie and taking her mind off the problem that had toppled her world. She even grudgingly forgave him for going out for Chinese food which Melanie had eaten with gusto.

"Mike, if you're finished, why don't you go across the street and relieve one of the boys so he can go get them something to eat. Then when they're settled in for the night, come back and check in with me."

"Sure, Lance. Ladies." Mike excused himself with his characteristic economy of words.

"What's across the street?" Erin's curiosity had gotten the best of her and she couldn't help but ask what she thought was a harmless question.

"Mr. Barrett's team has headquarters over there. They can watch this house, trace all the telephone calls, things like that. We mustn't ever answer the red telephone. All our calls on the regular house phone are being taped. Wasn't it lucky that the house was vacant just when they needed to rent it?"

Melanie's eyes were wide with excitement, but

Erin saw a flash of irritation in Mr. Barrett's. He was less than happy with Melanie's loquacious explanation.

"It's time for you to go back to the study, Miss O'Shea," he said peremptorily as he grasped her upper arm and virtually dragged her out of her chair.

"I think I should help Melanie with the dishes," Erin protested, as she tried to extricate her arm from his hand. It was a futile attempt.

"I'll help her," he said.

She stumbled down the hall after him, barely able to keep up with his long stride. When they reached the door of the study, she jerked her arm free and faced him belligerently. "Do you have to manhandle me that way?"

"Did I hurt you?" he asked quickly. Was that a touch of genuine concern she heard in his voice? His hand came back to her arm, but this time when he touched her, it was almost a caress, as if he were soothing the place that may have been bruised by his fingers only moments before.

She could feel the warmth of his hand through her silk sleeve as he stroked her arm. Tentacles of sensation radiated from his fingers and ran up her arm and curled around her heart, swelling it, expanding her chest. His hand was so comforting as he continued to gently rub her arm, that Erin had the strange impulse to lean against that hard, strong chest and seek even more comfort.

Wasn't there some study on the extraordinary relationship that developed between captives and

captors? Didn't captives often come to depend upon
their captors to the point of love?

That possibility seared her brain and shook the
foundations of her soul. She stepped away from
him, suddenly afraid of the very real physical threat
he posed. She must have imagined that momentary
gentleness on his part, for when she looked into his
face, it was hard and set in the grim lines she had
come to recognize.

She heard him mutter a curse as he turned around
and stalked down the hall.

CHAPTER

Four

Erin was leafing through photograph albums when
Lance came back into the room several hours later.
It was not quite eleven o'clock, but her body was
working on Houston time, and in light of the events
of the day, she was exhausted. Somehow though,
she couldn't lie down on the sofa and seek the oblivion of sleep.

She pored over the pictures in the albums, searching each one for revealing traits of her brother's
personality. Melanie had brought her the albums
when she had carried in an armload of blankets and
pillows.

"Mr. Barrett asked me to bring these things to
you. I offered to let you sleep in the guest bedroom
upstairs, but he said no."

"That figures," Erin grumbled.

"I remembered these albums were stored in our

bedroom closet. Would you like to look through them?"

"Thank you, Melanie. I can't tell you how boring these four walls have become. Besides, I want to learn all I can about Ken."

Displaying an understanding that surprised Erin, Melanie said, "I'd love to stay and talk to you, but I think I should leave you alone. There are over thirty years of Ken's life that you need to catch up on."

Impulsively Erin went toward her sister-in-law and kissed her on the cheek. "Thank you for accepting me. I know that when they find Ken, everything will work out for the two of you. I'll be available if you need any help."

"Oh, Erin, Ken is going to love you. I know he is." She sounded like an innocent child again.

Erin took her shoes off and curled her feet under her as she sat in the corner of the leather sofa and began studying the photographs. There were pictures of Ken with a nice-looking couple whom Erin supposed to be his adoptive parents. She laughed over one photograph featuring a Ken about nine years old wearing an enormous pair of Mickey Mouse ears standing outside the gates of Disneyland. For the next brief hours, his whole life kaleidoscoped before her eyes. She reached out and touched a recent photograph taken on Fisherman's Wharf. Ken's dark hair was windblown, his smile rakish, his long legs in the ragged cutoffs were tanned and muscular.

Tears pricked the backs of her eyelids as she prayed that soon she would see this man who was the only person on earth she knew of with whom she shared a bloodline. With the back of her hand, she whisked away the tears as the door opened and Lance walked in.

He stood in the doorway for a moment and allowed himself the luxury of staring at the woman folded into the corner of the couch. *Either she's who she says she is, or she's one hell of an actress,* he thought grimly when he caught her brushing away the tears.

Her fatigue was all too evident as she looked up at him, but he thought the hollows under her cheekbones added a waifish quality to her face that was beguiling. The faint lavender shadows under those wide, fathomless eyes made them even more haunting. Any man with an ounce of sense would run as far and as fast as he could from them.

He swallowed the lump that unexplainably formed in his throat when he noted the slender legs tucked under her hips. Her skirt had ridden up over the knee and accommodated him with an unrestricted view of a smooth, slim, silk-encased thigh.

Hell! he thought. If he didn't know the muscles of his face were frozen into that implacable mask, he'd be making a fool of himself. He felt like a schoolboy seeing his first copy of *Playboy*. He wished he didn't remember how her mouth tasted.

"Mr. Barrett?"

Her hesitant question brought him to the surface again. Maybe his face hadn't been as unreadable as he imagined. "I thought you might already have been asleep," he said, closing the door behind him.

"No. I'm tired, but the day has been too tumultuous, I guess. I don't seem to be able to relax." The sight of him hadn't done anything to calm her. If she gave credence to her senses, his presence in the small room had increased her anxiety.

"Would you like something from the kitchen?"

"No. Thank you." His civility was as unnerving as his former hostility.

She watched him warily as he took off the necktie that had been loosely knotted all day. He draped it over the back of a chair. Then he put both his palms to the small of his back and stretched, expanding his chest out in front of him. The play of muscles under his shirt was awesome. Finally, he released his breath in a long expulsion of air, and the muscles returned to their normal state.

"Which blanket do you want?" he asked as he sat down in a deep overstuffed chair. With the toe of one foot, he pushed the heel of his loafer off the other foot.

Staring at him, disbelieving his intention, Erin stammered, "You can't mean—I—you're not—this is—"

"Could you be a little more specific, Miss O'Shea?" he asked sardonically.

His teasing made her furious. "You're not thinking of sleeping in that chair?"

He looked at the chair he was sitting in as if weighing its merits. "Well, I was planning to. But if you'd rather I join you on the couch—"

"You stay where you are," she commanded, pointing an imperative finger at him as he moved to get out of the chair. "What are you trying to pull?" she demanded as she stood and took two steps toward him with her balled fists planted on her hips. "You must have a James Bond hangup, thinking you can bully a woman all day and then seduce her at night. Well, I'm informing you now, Mr. Barrett, that unlike those libidinous females in the movies, I *can* and *will* resist you."

"You're making far too much of this, Miss O'Shea," he said quietly and reasonably. Her tirade sounded ridiculous. "Rest assured that my reasons for sharing this room with you are strictly professional. Believe me, I'd rather be across the street stretched out on the bed I've been using for the past ten days than sleeping in this chair."

"I don't require constant surveillance," she flared.

Again his voice was annoyingly calm. "Probably not, but until I can confirm your identity, you stay under my watch. I wouldn't want to allow a gunrunner or drug dealer to escape into the night."

"Oh, for Pete's sake!" she groaned, rolling her brown eyes heavenward.

She flopped down on the couch in irritation and sulked for a moment while he began sorting through the blankets and pillows. His every movement attracted her attention and she couldn't help but stare. If she would admit it, the idea of spending the night in the same room with him was exciting. She wasn't nearly as irritated with him as she was with herself for the outrageous pounding of her heart and the murmurs of arousal that stirred her as never before.

When he had divided the linens equally, he turned around to face her. Her disparaging expression was well-known to her employees. It usually portended bad news for someone who had made a stupid mistake. "I would like to take a shower."

"Forget it."

"I need to go to the bathroom!" she exclaimed.

"*That* I'll allow."

"How kind," she cooed. She pushed past him, picked up her two bags, and marched toward the door. "Lead the way, warden," she said.

His golden eyebrows lowered menacingly over the piercing blue eyes, but he didn't remark as he opened the door and showed her down the dim hallway to a tiny half-bath under the stairwell.

"Feel free to put on something more comfortable," he said. He was standing close and they were almost in total darkness. Without the benefit of her high-heeled shoes, he loomed over her, and Erin's knees suddenly seemed to lack the strength to support her. They trembled with the exertion.

In defense of her own uneasiness she said, "You'd like that, wouldn't you?" She had intended her words to sound like an accusation, but to her dismay, they came out like a suggestion.

He took one step closer and she could feel his breath sweeping her upturned face, though the darkness obscured his features. He continued to incline toward her until he trapped her between him and the wall. His body was as rigid and tense as hers. It was like being pressed by a statue.

But the statue came to life.

The clay had not yet been baked to its rock hardness. Instead, it was still being molded—against her. It took shape by adjusting its form to hers until it was a perfect, complementing fit.

From the corner of her eye, she saw him raise his arm, and she thought that he was about to embrace her. But his outstretched hand flicked on the light switch in the bathroom behind her.

The sudden brightness dispelled the moment that seemed to have lasted for a small eternity. She turned away quickly and maneuvered her bags through the door of the bathroom.

"Don't take too long or I'll come in there and get you."

"Aren't you going to leave?" she asked in horror as he leaned against the doorjamb.

"Un-huh," he said, shaking his head.

Her lips compressed in fury, and she deliberately slammed the door in his mocking face.

She dropped her luggage on the floor and supported herself against the lavatory with stiff arms.

Drawing several deep breaths, she closed her eyes and tried to wipe out the vision of his face. It swam before her and she continued to tremble even as she turned on the cold water faucet.

He was a brute. Obnoxious. Unfeeling. Yet here she was, acting like an idiot, shaken and disoriented after one brief contact with him. She had actually wanted him to kiss her again. God forbid!

Still, she couldn't help but wonder what his lips would feel like in a tender kiss. The one he had given her earlier today had been a test. He had wanted to see how far she would carry her "brother" story. The kiss had been fierce and hard. But for one millesimal of a second, when his tongue had ceased to lash the hollows of her mouth, paused, and then merely touched the tip of her tongue, hadn't she discerned an instant of sweet tenderness?

No! she thought as she brushed her teeth with a vigor hopefully strong enough to rid her mouth of every lingering trace of him.

She creamed her face and brushed her hair. It was no small task to open out her larger suitcase in the small space, but she managed to open a narrow wedge wide enough for her hand to explore its contents.

By feel, she located a pair of jeans and a T-shirt. The jeans weren't the designer brand she usually wore starched and stiff. This pair was old and faded and laundered into softness. With much twisting and turning, she managed to get out of her wrinkled suit and pull on the jeans.

For a moment she deliberated about taking off her bra. She hated to sleep in one all night, so she unclasped it quickly before she could change her mind and sighed in relief at the freedom. Even though she had crossed the confidence-shattering line from her twenties on her last birthday, she knew that her model's figure was still firm enough to forsake a bra now and then. Tonight it wouldn't matter.

When she pulled the T-shirt over her head, she saw that since its recent washing, it was slightly tighter. It *did* matter that she hadn't left on her bra. Her breasts looked far too impudent and eager to go without one. Sighing, she grasped the hem of the shirt and was about to take it off when Lance knocked on the door.

"Time's up," he said tersely.

"I'll be out in a minute. I'm almost fin—"

Before she could complete the sentence, he opened the door. For a moment, with her arms crossed over her chest and the bottom of her shirt raised, he caught a glimpse of the smooth expanse of her stomach and the merest hint of two crescents under soft pink cotton.

Erin pulled down the T-shirt. As though drawn by a magnet, his eyes riveted on her breasts. She could feel her nipples, hard and tingling, straining against the fabric. For years, before she was married to Joseph Greene and working as a house model, she had stood practically nude for hours at a time while designers and seamstresses made alterations.

Never had she felt this self-conscious, this aware of her own body.

Forcing down her sudden attack of modesty, she cried, "You are unbelievably rude! I told you that I needed a few more minutes."

Lance was finding it difficult to talk. His brain didn't seem capable of transmitting the correct message to his tongue. He gulped and said with as much severity as he could muster, "And I told you that time was up."

"Will you at least let me take a pill? I missed one today." She was fishing in her makeup bag, willing her hands not to shake so visibly. She found the package of penicillin and pushed a tablet out of the foil backing. There was no glass, so she tossed the pill down her throat and then cupped several handfuls of water into her mouth, swallowing the tablet with difficulty. When she straightened, she saw Lance in the mirror, staring at her hips as she leaned over the sink. He hurriedly averted his eyes and mumbled, "You can leave your things in here if you want to. No one will bother them." He walked softly down the hallway in his stockinged feet.

His suggestion was accepted without a comment from her. She'd leave her suitcases in the bathroom. He wasn't gentlemanly enough to offer to carry them for her, and she felt drained of the energy or will to carry them herself. It was easier to not argue with him, to switch off the light, and to simply follow him meekly down the hallway to the paneled study.

Desultorily she entered the room and saw that Lance had turned out all the lights except one small lamp on the table beside his chair. She spread out one of the blankets on the leather sofa, placed a pillow in the corner of it, and sat down, stretching her legs along the couch and covering them with another blanket.

Lance waited patiently, staring moodily into space, not speaking. He made no effort to turn off the light and Erin couldn't lie down while it was still on. That would make her too vulnerable, too exposed. Trying hard not to look at him, she glanced around the room, an occupation that had filled most of the afternoon.

"There has never been a fire in that fireplace," she remarked idly.

Lance didn't move his head, but his eyes shifted toward her. "What?"

"Did you notice that there has never been a fire in the fireplace? It has a lovely carved wood mantel, the logs are stacked, but there is no soot on the bricks. I can't imagine having a fireplace and never lighting a fire in it."

"That's a very keen observation. Maybe you should have gone into my line of work." She looked across at him to see him smiling at her from his slouched position in the chair. Without having to think about it, she smiled back. "Do you have a fireplace?" he asked.

"Three."

"Three?"

She laughed at his astonishment. "Yes. I live in my parents' house, the one that I grew up in. When Dad died, Mother wanted to sell it. I begged her to lease it for a while, and she did for several years. Then when I left New York and came back home, I moved into it. It's modest, but very old and full of character. I've redecorated and refurbished it."

"Sounds nice."

"Most people would never give it a second look, but to me it's home. I guess when you've been adopted, it's very important to establish family traditions, things like that. It's almost an essential part of your life to secure an identity."

They were quiet for a long moment and then Lance asked, "The O'Sheas, they were good to you?"

"They were wonderful parents. No one could have asked for better. Dad was tall and robust. He always seemed huge to me, even after I was grown. He was the gentlest man I've ever known, despite his size. He was a carpenter. Mother is petite, spunky, and has laugh lines around the bluest eyes you've ever seen." *Besides yours,* she added to herself.

He stretched his arms high over his head while he yawned broadly, then raked his fingers through the gilded brown hair. "You'd better get some sleep. Good night," he said as he switched off the light.

"Good night."

She shifted down between the blankets until she

was lying on her back, staring into the darkness. She could hear Lance making himself as comfortable as he could in the chair. There was a rustle of covers, a deep sigh, then silence fell over the room.

After long, silent minutes, knowing instinctively that he wasn't asleep, Erin whispered, "Mr. Barrett?"

"Hm?"

She plucked at the blanket with nervous fingers. The darkness lent an intimacy to the situation. Like lovers after . . . "What will happen to my brother when you find him?"

Sounds of him changing his position in the chair reached her out of the darkness. His voice was low, hesitant . . . sad? when he answered, "I don't know. That's beyond my realm of expertise. He embezzled a tremendous amount of money from a national bank. The theft alone would be enough to keep him incarcerated for years. The federal government gets sticky about someone taking its money."

"He'll have to go to prison," she said without emotion. It was a mere statement of fact. She hadn't thought of it before now.

"Yes. It may help that his father-in-law is president of the bank. Winslow didn't call in the local police, though we're using some of their men who are trained to find needles in haystacks, so to speak. Maybe if Lyman hasn't spent the money and can return it, he'll only be slapped with a stiff fine and a long probation."

"You don't really think that, do you?"

His voice sounded tired and resigned when he said, "No." Moments later he said, "In all my years of doing this kind of work, I've never understood the criminal mind."

"My brother is not a criminal!" she cried.

"He committed a crime. By definition that makes him a criminal," he reasoned.

She drew a deep sigh of remorse. "Of course you're right. I'm sorry. What were you saying?"

"Well, it looks to me like he had so much going for him. Why did he do it? Why did he risk everything? Leave Mrs. Lyman? It was a dumb, stupid thing to do. He must know we'll catch him."

Erin was surprised to hear the anger in his voice. It was almost as if he wished he didn't have to find Ken. "Melanie will be so terribly hurt by all of this. I don't think she realizes the gravity of the situation."

"She doesn't. She's a sweet kid. We could have set up our base of operation anywhere, you know. We're here partly to protect her. We don't know if Lyman was working alone or if he was involved in something bigger. She may become the innocent victim of someone seeking revenge. Hell, I don't know." His exasperation with the case was all too clear, and Erin felt a pang of contrition for having added to his headaches.

Softly she asked, "What about me? Do you think I'm an unlikely-looking assassin that came in with a sob story to win the affection of a vulnerable girl and then murder her?"

There was a significant pause before he admitted, "It crossed my mind."

"I see," she whispered.

Her head was whirling with all he had told her, but it seemed too light to remain on the pillow. She tossed restlessly on the narrow space of the sofa, trying to find a comfortable position that would allow her to drift into a much needed sleep. Finally, annoyed with her insomnia, she lay on her back and flung her arms over her head.

Was it the soft swishing of clothes or the popping of his knees as he crouched down beside the sofa that first alerted her that he was no longer in the chair? She didn't know. All she knew was that he was suddenly so close that she could feel the heat emanating from his body. She lay utterly still, not even daring to blink.

"I don't know who you are, or what you are, but you're not an assassin." His voice was husky with emotion, but she barely had time to analyze it before she felt the brush of his lips across hers.

Did a small sigh of pleasure escape her lips? Did she turn her head in a gesture of entreaty? What made his lips linger, hovering over hers for a heartbeat before melting against them and claiming total possession?

The cloak of darkness that enveloped them extinguished the hostility, the wariness, the suspicion, the resentment that had sprung between them. In that black velvet cocoon where no judgments are made and secrets are kept, they lost their identities.

The differences between them seemed petty, indeed
they ceased to exist. They were only two people,
equalized by a need, seeking fulfillment for a longing as puissant as it was indefinable.

Erin's lips were sweet and tender beneath his and
parted in anticipation. He tasted, savored, memo-
rized her with his lips and teeth and tongue until she
breathlessly sighed his name.

Of their own volition, her arms lowered, and her
hands clasped the sides of his head. He trailed hot,
fervent kisses along her neck. His hands settled on
her rib cage, almost encompassing it with their wide
span. Tantalizingly she felt his thumbs move to the
undercurves of her breasts and stroke them lightly.

She entwined her fingers in the thick golden hair
as his face oscillated between her breasts. Moist
breath scorched her skin through her T-shirt. With
her help, he removed that last barrier. His fingers
delighted in the texture of her skin and sought to
explore every inch of it from her neck to her waist.

Then he kissed her, once on each breast. Completely covering the tip with his mouth, he flexed
his cheek muscles. As though they were connected
by an invisible cord, she felt that sweet tugging on
her nipple deep in her womb. It caused a tiny vol-
cano to erupt inside her, filling her veins with mol-
ten lava and bathing her body with its own liquid
fire.

"Oh God." His moan was born of the agony of
self-denial. He covered her breasts with his palms.
His lips came down on hers once again. His fero-

cious hunger was tempered only by a desire to bring her as much pleasure as he found in the kiss. Though his tongue coaxed her to kiss in a way she had never kissed before, it was a gentle persuasion.

All too soon, he raised his head. She could feel his stare. His features were indistinguishable in the absolute darkness, but his eyes were powerful even without the benefit of light. She was held immobile and silent under that hypnotizing power.

"This never happened," he rasped. "Do you understand, Erin?" His voice was urgent, compelling her to grasp what his words conveyed. "This never happened. *Do you understand?*"

Dumbly she shook her head "no."

But of course, in the darkness, he couldn't see her.

CHAPTER
Five

He had already left the study when she woke up. She opened her eyes slowly and, without moving her head, surveyed the room. It hadn't changed overnight. Everything was exactly as it had been before. Only she was different. All the changes had been within herself.

What had she done? How had it happened? What had she been thinking? Obviously she *hadn't* been thinking or it would never have happened. Had she gone temporarily insane?

Maybe it had been a nightmare. Yes? No.

All right, if it were too pleasant to have been a nightmare, maybe it had been a dream. No. She could still smell elusive traces of Lance's cologne on her skin. Her breasts were slightly abraded where whiskered cheeks had nuzzled her. Her body evidenced too many signs of his intimate embrace.

Even now she could recall each nuance of it in vivid detail. It had been no dream.

Her eyes wandered again to the chair where he had slept. The pillow crumpled in the corner still bore the imprint of his head. A feeling of great tenderness welled up inside Erin, and she caught herself smiling in remembrances.

The smile vanished when she saw his blanket lying discarded on the floor beside the chair. No doubt he had discarded thoughts of her just as indifferently.

She covered her mouth with a dainty fist. Mortification caused her eyes to squeeze tightly shut when she recalled the abandon with which she had kissed him back. God! He must be basking in self-satisfaction this morning. Surely he would be very pleased with himself. He could have easily seduced her to . . . No!

Another sob rose in her throat and a tear managed to slide past her closed eyelids and roll down her flushed cheek before she buried her face in the pillow.

How had it happened?

She couldn't defend herself by saying that he had plied her with alcohol, or played on her sympathy, or physically forced her to submit to his kisses. He hadn't even wooed her with loving words. He hadn't said anything. He had merely come to her out of the darkness and touched her and kissed her and she had been more than willing to give him even more than he had demanded.

Miserably, she moaned again with the humiliating recollection of how her naked breasts had been plundered by his greedy mouth. No. His mouth had been neither plundering nor greedy. To add to her abasement, each time her mind conjured up the memory, her body ached again with longing.

She mustn't lie here and dwell on it any longer. It would be better to face him with an aloof attitude. It had been nothing more to him than a naughty game in the dark. She wouldn't let him know that it had meant more than that to her. Getting off the couch, she realized her breasts were still bare. She found her T-shirt behind the sofa after a frantic search.

She crept on silent feet toward the door. Listening thoroughly, she couldn't hear anyone else in the house stirring. She left the study and went into the tiny bathroom she had used the night before. She shuddered with embarrassment when she remembered Lance catching her in that awkward position with her shirt raised. In fact, any thought of Lance Barrett brought on a wave of hot sensations.

"Oh, there you are," Melanie said as Erin came out of the bathroom. Her sister-in-law was standing in the doorway of the study.

"Good morning," Erin mumbled, hoping Melanie wouldn't detect some sign of guilt.

She was behaving like a moron! After all, what had actually happened? A little heavy necking; that's all. People did it all the time. She wasn't a candidate for a scarlet letter. Yet.

"I've come to rescue you," Melanie said mysteriously. "I've persuaded Mike to let you come upstairs and take a long bath. Then you and I will have breakfast together."

"What about General Barrett? Don't you think he'll consider me AWOL?"

"Maybe he won't find out," Melanie trilled. "He's not here. Come on."

Melanie allowed Erin only enough time to pick up her suitcases in the bathroom, offering to carry the larger one herself, before virtually dragging her upstairs and showing her to the small, but comfortable, guest bedroom.

It was furnished in white wicker which contrasted nicely with the apple green walls. The bedspread and curtains were gaily scattered with a daisy pattern. A green and white striped easy chair was placed at an angle in a corner.

"The bathroom's through that door," Melanie said. "I checked everything, but if I've missed something you need, just call me."

"Thank you, Melanie. It's lovely. Really. I'll be down as quickly as I can."

"Don't hurry on my account," Melanie said.

"I'm not. I'm hurrying on Mr. Barrett's account."

Melanie only giggled before she closed the door and left Erin alone.

The bath was heavenly and she reveled in the hot, bubbly, scented water. She convinced herself that she took no special pains with her appearance this morning, but the results of her efforts made it seem otherwise.

She blew-dry her hair, skillfully wielding the hairbrush to produce a style of artful disarray for her dark curls. She chose a khaki skirt and a cotton plaid blouse in muted shades of blue and burgundy. Her Beene Bag shoes were navy kid with stack wood heels. Her only jewelry besides a tailored gold wristwatch and Bart's diamond ring was a pair of small gold loops in her ears. She looked cool, confident, and in perfect control.

That control slipped when she heard Lance Barrett's voice coming from the kitchen as she was descending the stairs. Her heart jumped to her throat and she gripped the banister reflexively when her footsteps faltered.

"Hey, Lance, is that you?" She recognized Mike's voice.

"Yeah."

"Charlie Higgins is holding on the line for you."

"Be right there."

Erin could hear hurried footsteps as Lance journeyed through the house toward the living room. What would he say to her this morning? What would she say to him? Not for one minute did she believe that he could have forgotten what they had shared in the inky darkness despite his commission for her to do so. How could she ever forget those few precious minutes when she experienced total bliss from a man's embrace? She still felt the impact of his lovemaking like rippling aftershocks to an internal earthquake.

She had to face him sometime, so it might just as well be now. She took the last few steps down the stairs and then stood poised on the bottom stair where she could see into the living room. Lance held the telephone in the crook between his clefted chin and his shoulder. He was jotting down notes on a tablet.

She had expected him to look like he had the day before—gray slacks, dark tie, white shirt, the uniform of all government officials. That was hardly the sight that greeted her eyes.

Lance was clad only in a brief pair of blue running shorts and a pair of running shoes. Nothing else. As he leaned over the desk, writing on the paper that was becoming soggy from the sweat on his hand, he grew impatient with the glasses that continued to slide down his perspiration-beaded nose. In exasperation, he reached up and jerked them off, tossing them onto the desk as he continued to write furiously.

For how long she stood there and stared at him, Erin didn't ever remember, so mesmerized was she by the symmetrical perfection of his physique. Now she knew why he was in such superior physical condition. If he ran like this every morning—and by the looks of him, it had been no small distance—his secret to that well-honed body was out.

His legs and arms were hard and sinewy. His

shoulders were broad and topped an impressive chest that was matted with light brown hair now curled into wet ringlets. Erin's eyes shamelessly followed the growth pattern of that hair over a corded rib cage and a flat, taut stomach into the elastic waistband of his shorts. It was disconcerting that his deep tan showed no lines of demarcation. Even more unsettling was the full evidence of his sex beneath the tight, damp shorts.

"No, I think that should do it," he was saying crisply. "If I need anything else, I'll call. Thanks, Charlie. I owe you one."

He hung up the telephone and continued to scratch the pen across the paper for a few seconds before he straightened up.

He almost did a double take when he saw her watching him from the staircase. Then his eyes boldly traveled the length of her body and back up again. For a flickering moment their eyes met and locked and Erin's breath caught in her throat. She was perplexed when he looked away quickly. Where was the smug, knowing jeer she had expected?

Bravely she entered the room and stood in front of the desk. Finally, he raised his eyes and looked at her with a blank, unreadable face. "You're up early."

"So are you," she said. "Do you always start the day this way?" she asked, indicating with a nod of her head his postrunning condition.

"I try to get in several miles each day, yes." Why

were his sentences so abrupt? He wasn't engaging in conversation with her, he was answering her question out of politeness. His eyes told her nothing she wanted desperately to know.

"Wasn't it cold outside?"

His shrugging shoulders set all sorts of muscles into play, and Erin strove to tear her eyes away from his chest. "Sometimes it is when I start out, but I warm up fast enough. I had on a jacket. I left it out on the porch. The boys across the street said that Mike needed me."

He wiped the sweat out of his eyebrows with the back of his hand and attempted to dry it on his shorts. His movement was mechanical, for it was obvious that his mind was on something else.

"You'll be glad to know that your identity has been confirmed."

He said the words offhandedly, as if they weren't really important. She looked at him in surprise, but the rigid planes of his face remained intact. "I called a cohort in Houston last night and he got right on it. What he couldn't do last night, he followed through with this morning. We know everything there is to know about you, Miss O'Shea."

His reverting back to the formal means of address hurt her to the quick. Last night, just before he returned to his chair, he had whispered her name in the darkness and the sound of it coming from his lips had thrilled her. He didn't even remember.

"We know that your garbage is picked up on

Tuesday and Friday. I hope you remembered to put it out before you left.''

Was that supposed to be a joke? She didn't think so because he wasn't smiling. He wasn't looking at her either. His eyes darted around the room, studying first one object then another. If he looked at her at all, it was with a brief and sweeping glance. Since she had come in the room, he hadn't once met her eyes.

"You, of course, are free to go," he said matter-of-factly.

Why was he acting as though nothing had happened between them? Why didn't he smile, or tease, or torment? Why didn't he beg her forgiveness? Why didn't he do *something*?

"I'm sorry if I have inconvenienced you."

Perhaps if he hadn't said that last sentence, she would have left and remained forever bewildered by the enigmatic man she had once met in San Francisco. It was that casual dismissal that infuriated her. Her puzzlement turned into boiling anger and she lashed out at him.

"I guess everything you did was in the line of duty!"

He knew immediately to what she was referring, and Erin saw immediately that her anger was contagious. "Exactly," he said precisely.

Yesterday she had stormed at him for treating her with such abuse, but he hadn't even begun. Little did she know what degradation he had planned for her. Her eyes shone like burning coals as she glared at him.

"You—" she started.

"Mrs. Lyman is ready for you to come to breakfast. She's cooked up something special," Mike said, grinning as he came into the room.

He had interrupted Erin's well-chosen epithet and she felt robbed of the opportunity to blister the ears of Mr. Lance Barrett and shake his impregnable indifference.

"We're not here to eat," Lance snapped to the hapless Mike and his grin dissolved under the cold blue eyes.

"No, sir," he said quickly. "Only she's been cooking all this stuff and said . . ." He licked his lips nervously. Lance's stare hadn't relented one iota. Mike whipped the napkin out of his belt and asked, "Is there something you need me to do, Lance?"

Lance released a deep breath with a whooshing sound as he raked agitated fingers through the hair that was still sweat-plastered to his head. "No. Go on and eat breakfast. I'm going across the street to clean up. Then I need to make some phone calls to the main bureau, but if you need me, call. It shouldn't take me more than an hour."

With that, he came from behind the desk and stalked out of the room without once glancing in Erin's direction. She stood immobile for a moment, stunned and angry, until Mike said abashedly,

"Mrs. Lyman is waiting for you. I think I've had enough." He had been intimidated by Lance's overbearing attitude.

Lance Barrett had that kind of effect on people.

Melanie proved to be an accomplished cook, but all the while Erin was eating the sumptuous food Melanie had prepared, she was contemplating her future plans. She didn't know what to do.

Whether it was to her liking or not, she had become embroiled in her brother's life and he was in desperate trouble. He would never be the man he was before. He would either have to go to prison for many years or suffer some other stigma equally as devastating. Yesterday he had been no more to her than a name on a slip of paper, a hope, a promise. Today, he was a real person with real problems, and she couldn't turn her back on him, her only relative, when he would need all the support he could get.

Her reason for wanting to find Ken was that she longed for a family. What she had expected to find was warmth and happiness, hours filled with laughter and reminiscing. Instead she had walked into a tragic situation. Could that *negate* the fact that Ken Lyman was her brother? Families didn't always share joviality. They shared trouble, too. And perhaps that was far more binding.

She had become fond of Melanie. The younger woman's naiveté and sweetness evoked a maternal affection in Erin and she felt compelled to stay with Melanie and provide whatever help she could during the trying days still to come.

Her decision was made. She would stay in San Francisco.

As she absently sipped her second cup of coffee, she wondered why she felt no relief in having made that important decision. Could it be that she was worried about her business? Taking extended leaves of absence was no way to run a business, particularly one in which the clients often felt they needed to deal with her directly. They trusted Erin's expert opinion and imaginative, though excellent, taste. Sometimes they wanted her approval before they accepted a proposal presented by one of her employees.

Well, she hadn't missed more than a few days of work since she had started the business. She had trained her staff well. They would manage. And when one compared the problems that sometimes arose over a fashion show, they seemed far too trivial and superficial to weigh against the ones facing her brother and his wife.

Was it being away from Bart that made her hesitate in offering her assistance to Melanie? He would be peeved at her for staying in San Francisco. He would whine and plead for her to come home, but he would understand. She didn't intend to tell him about Ken's crime, but she would make her reasons for staying sound so imperative that a good businessman like Bart would see the advisability of her staying to find the solution to whatever problem detained her.

Melanie had been chattering gaily as she went about the chores of cleaning the kitchen after breakfast. She had insisted that Erin needn't help her. Erin hoped she was making all the correct responses to Melanie's questions and comments, but her mind still revolved around her dilemma. Why didn't she want to stay until Ken was found?

She knew the reason, but didn't want to face it. It was tucked away somewhere in her mind and she refused to bring it out of the safe corner into which she had hidden it.

Lance Barrett.

She didn't want to stay here with him around. It hadn't happened often in her life that Erin had been made to feel a fool. Her practical parents had taught her well to handle herself with aplomb, and she had never shied away from adversity, but rather met it head on.

How then could she have been so swayed by Lance last night? She should have fought him with all her strength when he first kissed her. She should have slapped his face hard, called Mike to her rescue, anything but lie there and respond so wantonly to his caresses. What had possessed her to behave that way?

She had resisted the advances of men since high school. And resistance had become more difficult and the advances more complex the older she became. Bart's persistent urging that she share his bed was an example of that. She had never allowed a man such access to her. Except, of course, poor Joseph. But that was totally different.

Still, Lance's attitude this morning was baffling. Just after he had switched off the light in the study last night, he had talked about Ken's future. He hadn't sounded as though he were speaking in an official capacity. He had sounded concerned. His kiss had been that of an ardent lover. Her body was no longer a stranger to his. He had spoken her name in an emotional whisper after that electrifying interlude in the darkness.

This morning he had reverted to that cool, impersonal demeanor and called her Miss O'Shea in that dictatorial voice. But he hadn't taunted her. He didn't look like a man pleased with himself. He seemed distraught and worried. She couldn't figure it out. Even though she had no illusions of him having any real romantic interest in her, she had expected some kind of reaction.

Even more galling was the fact that she found herself unable to forget his kisses. Though what had happened seemed to have had no effect on him, it had affected her. She had experienced sensations she hadn't known she was capable of until last night. Could she bear to stay in the same city with him, seeing him each time she came to visit Melanie? Her sudden involvement in Ken's life was staggering enough. She would be complicating matters a hundredfold if she became attracted to Lance Barrett.

The questions and arguments skipped and played

through her mind until she was ready to scream. And still she didn't know what course of action to take.

Meeting Melanie's parents convinced her of what she should do.

The couple rang the doorbell late that morning. Lance had not yet come back from across the street so Mike went to answer the door, after checking their identity through the draped living room window.

Erin, who was seated on the couch looking through a magazine, realized that Lance must have watched her before opening the door. She remembered waiting a long time for him to respond to the ringing doorbell.

Mike followed the couple into the living room and grumbled, "I'd better call Lance," before going to the red telephone and speaking into it. "Does he see them? Okay." He hung up and then said, "He'll be right over."

"We didn't come to see Mr. Barrett, and I resent not being able to visit my daughter without feeling like I'm being interrogated by that man."

The woman who had dressed down Mike so harshly was apparently used to getting her own way and never being subjected to anyone else's will. With a rueful smile Erin thought that indeed Lance would have been a shock to Melanie's mother.

She was a short woman whose figure necessitated moderation at the canape trays at cocktail parties. Her skin and hair were impeccably maintained. The dress she wore was casual, but Erin knew which designer's label was inside. Its price wasn't so casual, unless one were accustomed to having and spending a lot of money, which apparently Mrs. Charlotte Winslow was.

Howard Winslow was as well-groomed and stereotypical as his wife. His graying hair was closely trimmed around a patrician head. Had she not already known his profession, Erin could have guessed it at a glance. His dark blue suit, white shirt, and dark necktie indicated that he must have come straight from the bank of which he was president. His assurance, level steadfast eyes, and authoritative manner would imbue the customers of his bank with confidence and peace of mind that their money was well taken care of.

Erin disliked them intensely and immediately.

Melanie came skipping down the stairs when she heard her mother's voice and now she flew into the room, breathless and excited.

"Oh honestly, Melanie, I wish you'd let me make a hair appointment for you. That limp, straight hair is disgusting. Just because your husband has pulled this asinine stunt, do you have to let yourself go to seed, too?"

Erin was stunned by Mrs. Winslow's words. How could a mother speak to her child that way? Especially a child whose whole world had crumbled around her.

"I'm sorry, Mother. I haven't thought much

about my hair lately," Melanie apologized contritely. "Hello, Father."

"Hello, Melanie. Has there been any word from Ken?"

"Not directly," Melanie said mysteriously and grinned at Erin.

"What?" Mrs. Winslow demanded. "Was he found? Did he have all the money with him?"

"No, nothing like that," Melanie said dispiritedly. Her effervescence of a moment ago had been completely dispelled. "Someone came to see him. Someone very important." She gestured toward Erin, whom the couple hadn't deigned to acknowledge, though both of them had seen her when they entered the room.

"Well?" was Mrs. Winslow's only comment after she had given Erin a thorough inspection with her icy, colorless gray eyes.

"This is Ken's sister, Miss Erin O'Shea."

There was a heavy silence as Erin stood up politely to greet Melanie's parents. They stared at her as if she had been anathematized.

Before she had time to speak, the silence was broken by Lance opening the front door. *He really is exceedingly handsome,* Erin thought when he came into sight. His hair was still damp from a recent shower; his jaw was almost shiny from having just been shaved smooth. Erin could smell the brisk spiciness of his cologne from where she stood across the room. It was poignantly familiar to her.

At one quick glance he seemed to perceive the situation. Shoving his hands into his pockets in a careless gesture, he sauntered into the room. "Hello, Mrs. Winslow, Mr. Winslow. What are you doing here?"

"I'd think that would be apparent, Barrett," snapped Howard Winslow. "We haven't heard a thing out of you for the last few days and I demand to be kept well informed."

Lance's hands came out of his pockets slowly and Erin saw that they were balled into tight fists. His body was tense with dislike. Only his face remained passive. When he spoke, she was surprised by the level tone. "In the first place, Mr. Winslow, it isn't your place to 'demand' anything. It's not your money that's missing. It belongs to the federal government and the investors in your bank. Secondly, I told you I would keep you apprised of further developments. There have been none."

"Why not?" Mrs. Winslow flared. "It shouldn't be that difficult for you and your band of thugs to find one lone criminal."

"If you're referring to Mr. Lyman, let me point out to you that he hasn't been charged with any crime yet. All we know is that he and a large amount of money happen to be missing at the same time. I'd choose my words carefully if I were you, Mrs. Winslow. You never know when they may come back to haunt you."

Erin could have been knocked over by a feather when she heard what Lance said. Hadn't he said almost the opposite to her last night? He was defending her brother to these spiteful people and she wanted to embrace him out of gratitude. His disdain for the Winslows was as strong as hers. As he looked over their heads at her, she could see it in the blue eyes.

His voice maintained a level pitch when he said, "I see that you have met Mr. Lyman's sister."

Mrs. Winslow snorted, but her husband showed a trifle more courtesy when he said, "We had just been introduced when you came in. Am I to understand that you are a blood relative of Ken's? We were led to believe he had no family." The statement was rife with suspicion.

Bloodlines would be important to these snobs, Erin thought, but she said calmly, "Yes, Mr. Winslow, I am Ken's sister. He and I were adopted by different parents when I was an infant. When I learned of his existence several years ago, I began searching for him. It wasn't until a few weeks ago that I was convinced beyond a shadow of a doubt that Ken Lyman is my brother. I presented myself here yesterday to meet him."

Her eyes involuntarily focused on Lance who was still looking at her. Could anyone else feel the current that seemed to vibrate between them? "I was aghast when I learned from Mr. Barrett what sort of trouble Ken was in."

"I can't say that I was aghast when I heard about his thiev—" Mrs. Winslow broke off and darted her eyes fearfully toward Lance. "I wasn't surprised when he disappeared." she amended, though with venom. "I never trusted him. Not since the day I first laid eyes on him."

"Mother, please don't talk about Ken like that. He's your son-in-law." Melanie's voice was trembling and her bottom lip quivered. Erin resisted an urge to go to her and shield her from her vituperative parents.

"Through no fault of my own," the woman lashed out. Her eyes narrowed on her daughter and she shook a beringed index finger at her. "I told you you'd rue the day you married him. And I was right. And you'll go on regretting it for the rest of your life no matter what happens to him now."

Mr. Winslow also faced his daughter. "It wasn't only that he was too old for you. We didn't know anything about his origins, who or what he was descended from. I think his recent actions have proved our point."

Erin couldn't believe what she was hearing. How could anyone display such blatant rudeness? Didn't they realize how insulting to her their words were? She intended to tell them!

She took one belligerent step toward the couple and opened her mouth to scream her protests, but Lance stopped her.

Hurriedly he said, "If you don't mind, will you please postpone this family discussion until some other time? We have business to conduct. And I'll not tell you again not to come here. If Mrs. Lyman wants to see you, she can visit you at your residence.''

"Are you telling me to stay away from my own daughter's home?" Howard Winslow was appalled at the effrontery.

"Yes. I don't want it to look like a parade around here and scare off anyone who might be trying to contact Mrs. Lyman with information we could use."

"Well I never—"

Lance ignored Charlotte as if she hadn't started to speak. "I have the full cooperation of the San Francisco Police Department. If you show up on that front porch again, I'll call them and have you removed—by force if necessary. Leave. Now."

His stance and bearing brooked no argument. Mike, who had remained silent and invisible during the entire scene, now seemed to materialize and moved behind the Winslows as though he intended to shepherd them out the door.

Charlotte drew herself up and stared at him with open contempt, threw daggers at Lance with her steely eyes, and then marched through the door. Her husband, equally haughty, followed. The front door was slammed shut with such emphasis that the etched glass window rattled under the impact.

Erin heard Lance mutter an unspeakable obscenity under his breath. Mike stomped out of the room toward the kitchen. Melanie came running to Erin.

"Erin, I'm so sorry. They insulted you and I feel

terrible about it. I don't know what makes them so mean! And the way they talk about Ken, just— just," she burst into tears and turned to flee upstairs.

Erin cast a look toward Lance, but he didn't see her. He was sitting behind the desk, leaning on his elbows, his face hidden in his hands. She ran after Melanie.

She found the young woman sprawled across her bed crying like a teen-ager over her first unrequited love. Erin consoled her with words that were somehow supplied to her unconsciously. She was certain nothing she said made any sense, but whatever inanities tumbled out of her mouth seemed to help restore Melanie. She looked up at Erin with wide, disbelieving eyes.

"Did you say that you'll stay here with me until Ken is found?" She sniffed and wiped her nose with the back of her hand.

"If you want me to, Melanie."

"Oh yes, Erin. I need a friend who understands and shares my concern for him."

"I'll stay for as long as you need me." Her heart turned over when she saw the gladness and relief breaking across Melanie's tearstained face. "I'll find a room in a hotel and will only be a telephone call away."

"No, Erin. I want you to stay here with me. You're settled into the guest room. Please stay here. Please."

Erin gnawed her lip as she thought. Staying under this roof would put her in closer and constant contact with Lance, but Melanie's needs had to take precedence over her avowed avoidance of him. After witnessing how she was treated by her parents, Erin knew more than ever how lost her sister-in-law must feel.

"Okay," she agreed, trying not to let any of her reluctance show.

Melanie began planning all types of activities for them, but Erin urged her to lie down for a while and relax. Before she left her, Melanie was lying on her bed, breathing evenly, almost asleep.

When she walked in, Lance was alone in the living room. He looked up at her from the paper-strewn desk. For once his glasses were correctly positioned on the bridge of his nose and weren't clinging to another part of his head like some misplaced appendage.

"Is she all right?" he asked.

Erin moved into the room and collapsed into a chair opposite the desk. "Yes, although it's a wonder. I learned today that there is more than one form of child abuse. It's a miracle that Melanie's not a raving maniac."

"I agree. We've had to spend as much time fighting them and patching up their amateur attempts to do our job as we have spent doing our job." He almost smiled at his rambling sentence. "I'm going to try to keep them out of her hair as much as possible until this is settled."

"Good," Erin replied.

They were quiet for a moment and tried desperately not to look at each other. Erin knew from experience that her face was too expressive for her own good. She wore every emotion on her sleeve for all to see. That was particularly dangerous since Lance was so stoic.

After his eyes had taken several tours of the room, he said, "Tell me when you want to leave and I'll have Mike make your flight arrangements if you haven't already done so. I'll have him escort you to the airport, too."

"Thank you for your kindness, Mr. Barrett, but I'm not leaving."

CHAPTER
Six

Her words drummed into his ears and thundered in his head. He rebuked the surge of joy that raced through him. Most of the night and all day long, he had cursed himself for what he had done last night. That had been an incredibly stupid thing to do and he knew it.

He could justify that first kiss—maybe. He was putting a suspect on the spot to see how far she would go with a lie. But last night had been provoked by only one thing—lust.

He had told himself that when he saw her in the light of day, he would wonder why he had been so possessed by her last night. But it hadn't been that way. The moment he saw her this morning, that same desire had invaded him, constricting his muscles and making him strain against his clothes.

Now as he looked at her, he was drowning in those damn brown eyes, and his blood was running so high he wanted to hurdle across the desk and take her in his arms and kiss her until she was breathless. He wanted to taste her mouth again, to marvel once more at the texture of her skin, to see by light what he had caressed and kissed in darkness.

He wanted to hear again that deep, low purring sound that had come from her throat when he kissed her breasts. It hadn't been a noise that was rehearsed or conditioned, but rather was spontaneous and un-conscious.

This was madness! Whatever happened to his cold impersonality, his enviable objectivity? Love 'em and leave 'em Barrett. His conscience had al-most convinced him that one passionate kiss, one sensitive exploration would be enough, but it hadn't been. Not nearly enough. He wanted her, all of her, with a desperation he hadn't felt since adolescence. *It's impossible, Barrett!* Impossible.

Every time she came unbidden to his mind, he had comforted himself with the fact that she would soon be gone and he could start acting like a rational human being again. Now she was informing him that she wasn't leaving. Dammit! She had defied him at every turn. What made him think she would go all meek and obedient now?

He sprang out of the chair. "Like hell you aren't, Miss O'Shea."

She hadn't expected this strong a reaction from him at all, and for a moment she could only stare up at him with wide, questioning eyes, her lips

parted in surprise. She had no idea how utterly feminine and defenseless she looked.

Then her shock turned to anger and she stood up,
leaned over the desk, and met him head on. "I'm
not leaving. My sister-in-law needs me. You just
admitted as much not two minutes ago. What are
your objections to my staying here with her, Mr.
Barrett?"

"They are too numerous to name."

"You haven't got one valid one," she accused.

"I don't need one!" he roared, taking the glasses
from his nose and flinging them to the desk top. "If
I say you don't stay, you don't stay. I meant what
I said to the Winslows, and the same goes for you,
Miss O'Shea."

She stood upright and folded her arms across her
chest, tilting her chin back in an angle of challenge.
"You can threaten me all you want, Mr. Barrett,
but I'm not bullied easily. If you called the police
to have me bodily removed, I'd scream bloody murder. What do you think that would do to Melanie's
frame of mind? She's formed quite an attachment
to me. You'd have two hysterical women on your
hands. Besides that, I'm Ken's sister. That automatically gives me the right to be here."

She had him! She knew she had won by the way
he spun around on his heels, jerked at the knot of
his necktie, and strode to the window. Wise enough
not to press her point, she waited for him to speak.

"If you do anything to jeopardize this operation,

you're out.'' He still had his back to her, and when she didn't respond, he faced her. She nodded.

"Entertain Mrs. Lyman, keep her mind off her missing husband, and stay away from me.''

His arrogant conceit piqued her, but she curbed her sharp tongue. "I intend to,'' she said coolly.

"What about Billy Bob or whatever the hell his name is? Won't he be clamoring for you to go back to Houston?''

It took a supreme effort to control her fury. He knew damned well what Bart's name was. He never overlooked or forgot anything.

"Bart,'' she said bitingly. Then, "Yes, he'll be worried. I'll have to call him and my staff and explain that I'll be here for a while.'' She held up both palms when she saw he was about to interrupt. "I won't tell them why.'' She drew a deep breath. "If that's all, General, I'd like to return to the barracks.''

His lips compressed into a thin line and his glacial eyes were intimidating as he bore down on her with long, angry strides. "This may all seem like a big game to you, Miss O'Shea, but I assure you it's not. I'll not tolerate any sass from your smart mouth.''

His eyes went to her lips with the intention of reinforcing his command, but instead, the hard, imperious glare softened to an anguished plea. Erin noticed that his hands were clenching and unclenching at his sides. His eyes moved up from her lips across her nose and cheekbones to her own eyes. She melted under his fervent gaze.

The moment was so static with tension and suppressed sexual longing that both of them trembled under the assault of emotion. Each vividly remembered an incident better forgotten, but more treasured for its prohibitive, secretive nature.

Finally Lance tore his eyes away from her face and cursed under his breath as he went back to the desk and flopped down in the chair. "You can start now by leaving me alone. I've got work to do."

She didn't answer him, but left the room. Had she turned around, she couldn't have missed the painful longing nakedly revealed in his eyes as they followed her.

It was uncannily easy for her to adjust to the routine of the house. She used the telephone extension in Melanie's bedroom to check in with Spotlight as she had promised to do.

"Good afternoon, Spotlight," the bright voice answered.

Erin laughed. "I'd forgotten the time difference. It *is* afternoon in Houston, isn't it?"

"Hi there, stranger," Betty, her secretary, chortled. "Did you find who you were looking for?" she asked excitedly.

Even before Lance had intimated that she shouldn't discuss Ken's disappearance with anyone, she had decided not to burden her friends with her troubles. She answered, "Yes, I found him. Or at least I found his wife who has welcomed me with open arms. Ken is out of town for a few days."

"You mean he doesn't even *know* yet?!"

"No. We want to surprise him." Erin quickly changed the subject. "How are things there? Any major catastrophes I should know about?"

"No. Only a few minor ones we've managed to stumble through. You relax and have a good time."

"Betty, I may be here longer than I had anticipated. I expect you and the others to run the business as if I were there. I'm confident you can do it. But if you have any questions or anything out of the ordinary comes up, call me."

Betty paused for a moment before asking, "Are you sure everything's all right?"

"Yes. Positive," Erin lied. She gave Betty Melanie's telephone number and, after asking about the weather and everyone's health, hung up.

Unpacking her bags in the guest bedroom, she asked herself again if she was doing the right thing. Should she get back to her business and her life in Houston and forget about everything that had happened since her arrival in San Francisco?

No, she shook her head. She couldn't desert her brother and Melanie now that she had just found them. She had made a commitment to her sister-in-law and intended to uphold it no matter what unpleasantness she faced because of it, including Lance Barrett.

The rest of the afternoon she and Melanie spent in each other's company, talking for hours about Ken. Melanie knew quite a lot about his life before he met her and Erin realized that they must have a very happy marriage. But that was incongruous with the fact that he had stolen the money and abandoned her without a word. It was too complicated for her to figure out.

They strolled around the patio and backyard. Melanie was justifiably proud of her flower garden which she cultivated diligently. She named every shrub for Erin, explaining when she pruned, when she fertilized, how often she watered. Erin remarked that it must be a showplace in the spring when everything was blooming, and Melanie beamed happily.

It was amazing to Erin that the young woman, who had been born with a silver spoon in her mouth, would take such pleasure in cooking, keeping her house and yard, and shun her parents' life-style of country clubs and parties.

For dinner that night, Melanie baked a delicious quiche which they ate at the table in the kitchen. Lance and Mike had graciously declined her invitation to join them though she protested that she had prepared too much food for only two people.

Erin didn't see Lance again until late the following morning, and then it was quite by accident. She was having difficulty zipping up the back of the blue wool jersey dress she had put on. The soft fabric had gotten caught in the teeth of the zipper and no matter which way she tried to move it, the zipper wouldn't budge. She was on her way to ask Melanie for assistance when she bumped into Lance as she stepped out into the hallway.

"Oh!" she exclaimed in embarrassed surprise and backed against the wall, aware that her back was exposed.

"Hi," he said, as unsettled by their abrupt meeting as she was.

"Hi."

"I, uh, came up here to replace a light bulb for Mrs. Lyman."

"Oh." Erin felt imbecilic standing with her back against the wall that way, but she couldn't move without grabbing the shoulders of her dress and giving away her predicament. She was afraid it would slip down her arms.

"She's down in the kitchen," Lance said irrelevantly. Puzzlement was creasing the vertical line between his brows.

"I'll catch up with her down there. With your permission, she and I would like to go out for a while this afternoon. She wants to take me to Fisherman's Wharf."

"You want to go sightseeing?" he asked, scoffing.

"No I don't!" she bristled. "But Melanie wants to take me. It will do her good to get out of this gloomy house, the atmosphere of which you don't improve one bit."

"I'm not here in the capacity of court jester. Or have you forgotten my very serious reason for being here?"

Immediately she regretted her outburst. He must have a million details on his mind with the red telephone in the living room continually ringing. He didn't need her to contribute to his worries. "No. Of course I haven't forgotten," she said humbly. "Is it all right if we go?"

"Yes," he sighed resignedly.

She looked up at him and was held by the magnetism of his eyes as they stared down into hers. A fleeting impulse to reach up and investigate the cleft in his chin was stifled just in time. But there was no calming the frantic beating of her heart. She turned away quickly and took one step before the cool air on her back reminded her of the contrary zipper. She slammed into the wall again.

"What in the hell is the matter with you?" he asked.

There was no use pleading ignorance. She'd just as well explain why she was behaving like such a ninny. He would stand there all day until she did. "I'm having trouble with my zipper. I was about to ask Melanie to help me."

Instantly a grin tilted the corner of his mouth. He smiled lazily and leaned his shoulder against the wall only inches from her. His voice was seductive as he drawled, "She's busy. I, on the other hand, am available, willing, and able."

"No—"

"Let's see what the problem is." Before she could resist, he had turned her around. She flushed hotly when she knew that her whole back was revealed to him. The dress was fully lined, so she wasn't wearing a slip. The skin of her back was naked except for the thin satin strap of her bra. The zipper started in the middle of her hips, covered only by sheer pantyhose.

She shivered when she felt him slide his hands inside the dress and place them on the curve of her hips just below her waist. His fingers were warm as they pressed into her skin.

For a long moment neither of them moved, and there was silence except for the pounding of their hearts which each was certain the other could hear. At first Erin thought she was imagining the sensuous movements of his fingers, but they became very real when she felt them on the bare skin of her stomach. One hand rested on her rib cage, close . . . close . . . agonizingly close to her breast. The other slipped under the waistband of her pantyhose and investigated her navel with gentle fingers.

Don't touch her, Lance commanded himself, but his hands refused to obey. *This is insanity. Her fiancé is as rich as Croesus and you*—But God, she felt wonderful. *Don't torture yourself this way.* Reluctantly he returned his hands to their original position before their enrapturing foray.

"Move back just a little," he said huskily. She took two small steps backward and could feel his fumbling movements as he tried to extricate the fine material from the zipper. Finally she felt it come free.

His fingers seemed disinclined to pull the zipper upward and close the dress over her back. "Thank you," she muttered quickly when she knew he had reached the top.

"Just a minute," he said, placing restraining hands on her shoulders. "There's a doodad up here." He pulled her closer to him and leaned down over the back of her neck to better see the tiny hook and the thread eye in which to insert it.

His fingers were warm against her neck and his fragrant breath stirred the curls at the back of her head. He had already accomplished the task of fastening the hook, but she didn't move away.

He encircled her slender throat with the fingers of both hands and did something hypnotic to the base of her neck with his thumbs. She swayed slightly before surrendering to the temptation and leaning into him. Unconsciously, she adjusted her bottom against his hips. Hard thighs pressed into the backs of her legs.

His lips caressed her ear as he spoke. "Do you always smell so delectable?" One hand slipped under her arm, moved around her waist, and flattened on her stomach, almost covering it completely. With a slow, steady, inexorable pressure, he drew her tighter against him.

She felt rather than heard his ragged breathing at the same time as she was aware of a powerful stirring against her. *Oh, God,* she thought, *I shouldn't let—*

"Erin, aren't you ready yet?" Melanie called shrilly from downstairs.

Erin and Lance jumped apart. Erin tried to compose herself as she answered unevenly, "I . . . yes, I'll be right down."

"Okay, I'll wait in the car," Melanie shouted back.

Color stained Erin's cheeks and she was unable to meet Lance's eyes as she mumbled to the carpet, "Thank you."

Conspiratorially he leaned down, placed his lips against her ear, and whispered, "It was my pleasure."

She all but ran down the stairs.

Any other time, Erin would have delighted in the pulsating, cosmopolitan excitement of Fisherman's Wharf. She and Melanie strolled along the piers taking in the unique sights, sounds, and smells. Melanie pointed out the major points of interest. Erin shuddered when she saw the deserted island of Alcatraz. Its bleak, ominous walls rose out of the blue water of the bay like some gruesome, concrete leviathan. The Golden Gate Bridge, even at this distance, was awesome in its proportions. Melanie rattled off statistics about it like a tour guide.

They succumbed to the tantalizing smells of the sidewalk vendors and bought paper cups of shrimp fresh out of the vats of seasoned boiling water. They ate hungrily, decided they hadn't had enough, and ordered another serving each. They bemoaned their overindulgence, but it had just begun.

Melanie practically dragged Erin up the steep sidewalk to Ghirardelli Square. They strolled through the picturesque shops and, though they were still full from the shrimp, treated themselves to a hot fudge sundae at the Old Chocolate Manufactory.

Erin could barely breathe, she felt so stuffed. Too many more weeks in San Francisco and she'd return home roly-poly.

"Do you think I should go back and buy that dress?" Melanie asked as she scooped up the last syrupy spoonful of her sundae. Erin had persuaded her to try on a dress that had caught her eye in one of the boutiques they had shopped in.

"I think it was made for you, my dear," Erin parroted the sales clerk in a high falsetto voice, and they were reduced to a fit of giggles.

"Okay," Melanie said, standing up from the small round table in Ghirardelli's. "I'll go get it. You talked me into it."

They traipsed back through the throng of shoppers and sightseers toward the boutique. A company of sidewalk comedians caught Erin's attention and she said to Melanie, "If you don't mind, I'll wait out here for you and watch the performance."

"Sure. I'll be back in a jiffy," Melanie said before being swallowed up by the crowd.

Erin was so engrossed in the talented antics of the performers that she didn't really notice the man standing next to her before he said, "They're quite good, aren't they?"

She looked up into a friendly face, unmistakably British with its ruddy complexion. "Yes they are," she said, smiling.

"Are you a native of San Francisco?" he asked conversationally in his clipped, short phrases.

"No. I live in Houston, Texas. You are apparently a tourist just as I am," she said.

He chuckled. "I plead guilty. We're frightfully obvious, I'm afraid."

"Where do you live?" Erin asked him.

"Kent. Actually this is my second trip to the . . . colonies." He grinned engagingly, and Erin laughed. "This is my first trip to California, however, and I—"

He was rudely interrupted when someone elbowed his way between them and grasped Erin's arm painfully. "Excuse us, old chap," Lance said in a voice that was anything but neighborly.

Erin didn't have time to wish the English gentleman a pleasant trip before Lance dragged her away through the crowd. She murmured apologies as they shoved through the press, noticing that several people gave them withering looks. Lance's actions weren't exactly mannerly, but he seemed impervious to the crowd and his rudeness.

When he had gotten her out of the flow of traffic, he demanded angrily, "Where the hell have you been? Where is Mrs. Lyman? Who the hell was that man you were talking to?" With each question, the pressure on her arm increased until she almost cried out in pain.

"I'm not telling you one damn thing until you let go of my arm," she said.

He looked down at the tight fist gripping her

upper arm as if realizing for the first time that he even had a hold on her. He released her immediately. "All right," he barked, "where is Mrs. Lyman?"

"She's in a boutique buying a dress," Erin explained as she rubbed her arm in an effort to restore its circulation. "She tried it on earlier and went back just now to pick it up. I was waiting for her out here."

"Who was the man you were having so much fun with?" His eyes were as cold as his tone of voice.

Erin's dark eyes flashed in vexation as she cried, "I don't know! He was just a man, a very friendly, nice man. Someone you couldn't identify with," she added scathingly.

"You can cut the sarcasm, Miss O'Shea. My rudeness is a product of worry. You were gone for hours! Then when Clark called and said he'd lost you in the crowd—"

"You had us followed!?" she asked incredulously. "Of all the—"

"For Mrs. Lyman's protection only."

"Like hell." Erin saw Melanie coming toward them chatting to a man who was as nondescript as Mike. He was looking chagrined as they walked up. "I found her," he told Lance unnecessarily.

"Yeah. Thanks," Lance said dryly. Erin felt sorry for the young man when she saw the censure in Lance's eyes.

Melanie seemed oblivious to the tension as the

foursome wound their way back to Erin's car. "We're parked across the street. We'll follow you home," Lance said as he held the driver's door open for her.

"Yes, sir. Anything you say, sir." She saluted him mockingly and found smug satisfaction in the tight, angry lines on his face as he slammed the car door.

She sought further revenge by asking Melanie to direct her on the longest route home. It included Lombard Street, the crookedest street in the world, having seven curves in one block. The Mercedes took them with ease. The car Lance was riding in didn't fare as well.

With the first twinges of an upset stomach, Erin thought she must be paying for her eating binge that afternoon. Her altercation with Lance surely hadn't done her digestion any good. She went to bed pleading fatigue and didn't mention her stomachache to Melanie.

She settled down in bed and tried to sleep, but tossed restlessly before finally dozing off. Sometime after midnight she was awakened by severe stomach cramps. Every muscle in her body contracted against them and sweat broke out of every pore.

Her limbs felt weighted down with lead as she threw back the covers and staggered toward the bathroom. She barely had time to switch on the light and lift the cover of the commode before she was violently ill.

In her life she couldn't remember having an attack of nausea like this. She retched for what seemed like an endless amount of time. With each spasm, the cramping in her intestines took her breath away. Intense heat snaked up her spine, washed over her neck and head, penetrated her brain, and burned in her ears. Then she would shiver with cold. A clammy sweat bathed her body, making her night-gown cling to her like damp seaweed.

At last, when she felt like she had been turned inside out, she washed her face in the lavatory and, unable to stand upright, virtually crawled back to the bed. She collapsed on it, relieved that whatever had made her so sick had been expelled.

That wasn't the case, however. She was alarmed when only a few minutes later, she felt her stomach churning again. She bumped against the door in her dash to the bathroom, and it crashed into the wall. She was still in the throes of nausea when she real-ized that Melanie was standing there watching her, looking white-faced and terrified.

When Erin was able to look up, Melanie was gone. Once again she stumbled toward the bed and fell across it, exhausted and aching. She jerked in startled reaction when the door to her bedroom was flung open and Lance's silhouette filled the door-jamb. His eyes were wild, his hair was mussed, and he was shirtless. A pair of jeans had been hastily pulled on. They were zipped, but not snapped. Running shoes were on his feet, but the laces hung untied on the floor. Melanie cowered behind him, tremulous and frightened in her pink quilted robe.

Lance came quickly to the bedside and leaned over Erin, placing a palm against her forehead. His face had lost its guarded look and his eyes traveled over her body anxiously looking for signs of injury or pain.

"Erin? What's the matter?" This couldn't be Lance. It was someone who looked like him. Lance never sounded this gentle and kind. He had called her Erin, not Miss O'Shea. She loved the way he said her name. What had he asked her?

"I . . . I don't know." Her voice was low and weak and hoarse. She could barely summon up enough breath to whisper. "I guess I ate too much today. The shrimp was bad maybe. I don't—" She grabbed her stomach and jackknifed in pain as another cramp seized her.

"Dammit," she heard him mutter under his breath before he ordered, "Mrs. Lyman, call your physician and tell him you have an emergency. This is no ordinary stomachache. If he can't come immediately, find someone who will."

"He's a friend. He'll come," Melanie said. To Erin, her voice seemed to float from the dark end of a long tunnel.

She panicked when she felt the bile rising once again in her throat and clamped her hand over her mouth. Lance flung back the covers and swept her into his arms, one arm supporting her back, the other under her knees. He carried her to the bathroom and deposited her in front of the commode. She had no time to feel embarrassed before she vomited again.

When she was finished, she straightened up and leaned shakily against the wall. Lance, with a supportive arm around her waist, said, "Here. Swish your mouth out, but don't swallow it."

He clinked a glass against her teeth, and she took a mouthful of the solution. It was green mouthwash diluted with water.

She washed her mouth out and spit into the sink. How would she ever look this man in the face again? Wouldn't he always remember her in this ravaged condition? She couldn't think about it now. All she could do now was cling to him like a parasitical ivy struggling for survival.

He lay her gently on the bed and covered her with the blanket against her shivering. He was sitting on the edge of the bed, stroking the sweat-dampened hair from her forehead when Melanie came running back into the room. "He'll be here in a minute. He only lives a few blocks away. Is she better?"

"I think so," Erin heard Lance answer. "Go down to the kitchen and fill a plastic bag with ice. Bring it to me."

Erin didn't remember Melanie leaving or coming back, but in what seemed a few seconds, Lance was saying to her, "If you feel nauseated again, I'll put this on your throat. It may help." She nodded weakly, but couldn't open her eyes. Her lids were incredibly heavy. All her strength was concentrated in her right hand which gripped Lance's as if retaining the hold on him were a matter of life and death.

She must have slept, for the next thing she knew she was being shaken by a hand on her shoulder and a strange, new voice was coming at her from the end of the tunnel. "Miss O'Shea. Miss O'Shea. If you're going to get a man out of bed at two o'clock in the morning, the least you can do is greet him properly."

The face hovering over hers was as kindly as the soft-spoken voice. The doctor's hair was gray, his eyes a faded blue. "How are you doing? Did you get rid of it all?"

"I think so," she nodded.

"You have quite a tummyache from what I hear. Does it still hurt?" He had pulled away the covers and was probing her abdominal region with practiced fingers.

She pondered the question for a moment and then answered, "It feels hollow, but every once in a while it cramps again. Not as bad as before."

"Well, there's not anything in there to cramp now," he smiled. Now he was taking her blood pressure, counting her pulse, and pushing a thermometer under her tongue. "I'm going to ask you some questions. Just nod your head yes or no. Do you have frequent cases of this type of gastritis?"

No.

"Has an ulcer been diagnosed by a physician?"
No.

"Was there any blood in what you threw up?"
No.

"Are you pregnant?"

For some inexplicable reason her eyes flew to Lance, who was standing at the foot of the bed. He had put on a shirt, but it remained unbuttoned.

"Um?" the doctor asked again.

No.

"Are you taking any medication including birth control pills?"

She was about to shake her head "no" when she remembered the antibiotic. Yes.

"I'll get it," Lance said and went into the bathroom.

The doctor took the thermometer out of her mouth and looked at it. "Well, you certainly don't have fever. Your temperature is below normal," he said with a chuckle.

"It usually is," Erin said and hoped that the grimace on her face was at least the facsimile of a smile. "What is your name?" she asked.

"Andrew Joshua."

"Thank you," she found the strength to whisper, and he patted her hand.

"Let's get you well, then you can thank me."

He took the package of pills out of Lance's hand and pulled a pair of silver framed glasses out of his breast pocket. He read the information on the back of the box.

Erin looked at Lance. He had shoved his hands into the pockets of his jeans and was staring at her from his post at the foot of the bed. It never occurred to her to question his presence in the room while the doctor examined her. She was simply glad that he was there. Quite out of context, she noticed that the furrow between his brows was perfectly aligned with the cleft in his chin. He gave her a brief, reassuring half smile and the warmth from his eyes seemed to reach out and touch her. She wished she didn't know how frightful she must look.

Melanie was still nowhere to be seen.

"Ah, penicillin," Dr. Joshua said. "What are you taking it for?"

"A sore throat."

"When did you get it?"

"Last week. Tuesday I think."

"You've followed the directions exactly, taking three each day?"

"The day before yesterday I missed one at noon." She slanted a look at Lance.

"Did you make it up or just skip it?" the doctor asked.

"I skipped it."

"Well, do us all a favor and skip the rest of them, too. I think you've had an allergic reaction to the drug. It's a very good drug, but as you know, to someone who is allergic to something, even a good thing can be deadly."

"But I've taken penicillin all my life," Erin protested.

"This is a new synthetic variety. Something in its makeup and yours is incompatible."

"I had no idea," Erin murmured.

"Well now you do. Be sure when you get home to notify your doctor of what happened. I'll write up a report you can take back with you. How's the throat now?"

"It hasn't bothered me for the last couple of days."

"Good. Now I'm going to give you a shot to help you sleep and keep those cramps at bay. I'll also leave an antinausea medicine in case you have any more attacks, though I doubt you will or you would have had another by now. Eat light until you feel really hungry." She was revolted by even the mention of food, and Dr. Joshua laughed at her expression. "I'm sure you won't want anything for a while."

He gave her the shot in her arm while chatting about the Houston Oilers last season. He tossed the disposable syringe back in his black bag and said, "Unless you want a bad case of pneumonia on top of everything else, you'd better get up and let us change this bed. Slip into another nightgown, too."

She struggled to sit up, but her muscles felt like water and another cramp gripped her. "I'm sorry," she gasped breathlessly and fell back against the pillows.

Lance was around the bed in a split second. He lifted her as he had before and carried her to the bathroom. Dr. Joshua was calling down the hall for

Melanie to bring fresh linens when Lance set her down on the dressing table stool.

"I'll get you another nightgown. Do you want me to send in Mrs. Lyman?"

She shook her head. "No. I think I can manage if you'll toss a fresh one through the door. They are in the second drawer in the chest." The speech, short as it was, exhausted her.

Lance disappeared and she slipped the straps of her gown down over her shoulders and managed to work it over her hips and step out of it without standing up.

"Here it is," Lance called from the other side of the door as the soft cotton nightshirt came sailing toward her. "Can you reach it?" he asked.

"Yes," she said and wondered what he would have done had the garment been out of her reach. She flushed hotly, and it wasn't from her illness. She *knew* what he would have done. She shrugged into the sleeves of the nightshirt and tried to button it down the front. For her weak, rubbery arms, it seemed like a Herculean task.

"Call me when you're ready," he said from beyond the door.

"I'm almost . . . I . . . ." she trailed off weakly.

He came through the door and saw her listless arms hanging loosely at her sides. A look of great tenderness came over his face and he knelt down in front of her.

He buttoned the nightshirt from her breast to her knees with dispatch, as though afraid to prolong it.

As he reached the last button, he paused. In the next heartbeat, his cheek was pressed against her bare knees as his strong hands molded the backs of her calves. She wanted to reach out and touch the burnished hair that tickled her skin, but couldn't summon the strength. His hands moved up the backs of her legs, massaging the tired, useless muscles.

He raised his head and dropped a brief kiss on her knee before he secured the last button. Lifting her into his arms, he carried her into the bedroom. She was coming to look forward to the strong arms enfolding her and drawing her against that hard body.

She saw that the doctor and Melanie were still making the bed and talking in subdued tones. She was growing drowsy under the effects of the shot, and her head fell against Lance's chest when he sat down in the easy chair with her in his lap.

A delicious languor overcame her. The rise and fall of his chest was rhythmic under her head, and the hairs exposed by his open shirt teased her nose. Unconsciously, she snuggled down deeper in his lap and slipped her hand inside his shirt, resting it on the crisp curly mat.

She didn't even know when her fingers instinctively sought that small bud of flesh nestled in those curls or the anguished joy it brought Lance when she touched him so privately. Without word, without thought, a small deed communicated a heart's secret desire. Lance's hand followed hers, slipping under the fabric of his shirt to cover that smaller hand, pressing it against him as if he wanted her to become part of his flesh.

It must have been her imagination when she felt him bury his face in her hair. The murmured words she heard were indistinguishable, but rife with emotion. And the sweet brush of lips across her forehead was surely part of a dream. But whether it was her imagination or not, she wanted this feeling to last forever and mumbled a feeble protest when she felt Lance rise with her and cross to the bed.

He was gently spreading the covers over her when she heard Dr. Joshua say, "Let her sleep tomorrow as much as she wants to."

"Will she be all right?" Was it Lance who asked that question so anxiously? It must have been. Wasn't he the only man here except for the doctor?

"Yeah. She'll be okay. She'll feel like hell tomorrow, but by the next day, she should be on the mend. Call me if she's not."

Erin heard their good-byes and through half-closed eyes saw the light go out. But not everyone left. Someone was coming back toward the bed. She thought whoever it was lifted her hand and pressed it against a hard, whiskered cheek before bringing it to his mouth and planting a deep, moist kiss into its palm.

She wanted to know who it was. But she couldn't stay awake.

Besides, it was probably only her imagination again.

CHAPTER

Seven

Judging by the position of the sun through the windows, she thought it must be sometime in the afternoon when she awakened. She lay motionless, waiting for another cramp to squeeze her stomach, but nothing happened. The only symptoms that remained were a debility in every limb and a soreness in every muscle.

Turning over onto her side, she saw that someone had thoughtfully left an ice bucket on the bedside table. She opened it, took out two small cubes of ice, and placed them on her parched, starchy tongue. She was asleep before they had melted completely.

Late evening had shaded the sky to a soft purple when she woke up to the clatter of dishes. She rolled over and saw Melanie pushing through the open door carrying a tray.

"You're awake," she exclaimed happily. "I was

beginning to think you'd sleep forever, but Mr. Barrett said that under no circumstances were you to be awakened.''

"Melanie?" Erin croaked. What had happened to her voice? She cleared her dry throat and tried again. "Melanie, I'm so sorry to bother you this way.''

"Erin! Please don't offend me by apologizing. You couldn't help getting sick.''

"I know, but I've been such a bother to you. As if you didn't have enough on your mind.'' She struggled to sit up, but barely managed to prop herself against the pillows.

Melanie set the tray on the table. "I'm the one who should apologize.'' She glanced down at her clasped hands. "I couldn't help you last night. Ever since I was a little girl, I have been terrified of illness. Anytime I'm around someone who is sick, I take on their symptoms. Forgive me, Erin, for leaving you alone when you needed me.''

Erin took Melanie's hand in hers. "I was too busy to notice,'' she said and made the effort to smile. "I feel much better now.''

"Oh, I'm so glad. Mr. Barrett thought you may want some crackers and tea. He has been acting so strangely all day. Do you know what he did last night? He told Dr. Joshua that you were his wife. I didn't say anything. When he gets that fierce look on his face—you know the one—I would agree to anything he said.'' Melanie didn't notice that her sister-in-law's face had drained of what little color it had. She continued: "He said your stomach would be empty. Can you eat something without . . . uh . . . throwing up again?" she asked worriedly.

"I don't know," Erin said. The thought of food was still obnoxious, and now her hollow stomach was fluttering nervously after hearing what Melanie had said about Lance. However, this weakness was annoying. "I'll nibble them gradually."

Melanie sat at the foot of the bed and talked to Erin while she ate two of the crackers. Then she sipped the tepid tea to moisten her mouth.

"The red telephone has been ringing all day. I think something is going on, but so far Mr. Barrett hasn't told me anything."

"Maybe there's really nothing to tell," Erin consoled the younger woman, who looked so helpless and forlorn. Again Erin apologized for being unable to lend her physical support.

"You just get well so you'll be healthy when Ken does come home," Melanie said as she stood up. "Would you like to visit the little girl's room?"

Erin agreed that she probably should while help was available, and together they managed to get her to the bathroom. She washed her face, brushed her teeth, and used the commode. The trip back to the bed seemed an odyssey.

As she gratefully sank back into the pillows, Erin said sleepily, "Melanie, thank you for bringing the ice today. It was just what I wanted."

"I didn't bring it. Mr. Barrett did."

She closed the door behind her, and Erin was

left alone in the twilight-tinted room with only her thoughts for company.

It was amazing what a difference twelve hours could make in her condition. In the morning, she was feeling much stronger. Tentatively she put her feet on the floor beside the bed and stood up. She swayed, and the room spun crazily before finally coming to rest, but she walked to the bathroom under her own power.

She took a sponge bath in the sink and changed into a fresh nightgown. Her hair was matted to her head, but a brisk brushing helped restore it to its usual springy luster. She relieved her dry lips by applying a slightly tinted lip gloss to them. As a last touch, she splashed on a lemony scented cologne. Any heavier fragrance would have played havoc with her queasy stomach, but the cologne made her feel more like a human being. She must be feeling better; vanity was emerging.

She was sitting on the edge of the bed rubbing lotion on her hands when the door opened a crack and Lance peeped in. Her hands stopped in midair, and she stared at him over the space that separated them. The pale peach nightgown she had put on was a soft batiste, but not too sheer. From a lace-trimmed yoke, it buttoned primly down the front.

"Hi," he said.

"Hi."

"Are you going to live?" he asked, smiling.

She returned the smile. "I think so, though I wasn't sure I wanted to for a while there."

"You were very sick."

She averted her eyes, inundated with embarrassment when she remembered how sick she had been in front of him. "I want to thank you for being so helpful the other night. It couldn't have been pleasant for you." *Why did you tell the doctor that I was your wife?* she longed to ask. She continued to stare down at her bare feet. When he didn't respond, she raised her eyes to him.

"You don't have to thank me," he said. "I wish I could have spared you the suffering." They looked at each other for a long, tense moment when all the rest of the world seemed to disintegrate, leaving only the two of them free to be totally absorbed in each other. He forced himself to tear his eyes away from the beguiling picture she made and said quickly, "You must be starving. I'll fix you something, though don't expect haute cuisine."

"Don't go to any trouble. Melanie—"

"Has gone to her parents' house this morning," he finished for her. "Family business. Mike is manning the telephone. I'm at your service." He smiled, but it was a self-conscious smile. "I'll be right back," he said before he hurriedly left the room.

Erin climbed into the bed after straightening the covers as well as she could. She fluffed the pillows and lay back against them, once again feeling drained of energy. Her body still had a long way to go until she felt up to playing a set of tennis, she thought tiredly.

She was just about to doze off again when Lance came in with a tray. "The blue plate special this morning features hot cereal, dry toast, and iced tea," he said with a broad smile.

He smiled so seldom. Perhaps it was a good thing he didn't. When he did, he was disarming and captivating. A weakness that had nothing to do with her illness permeated Erin's body. The nightgown over her breasts vibrated with the rapid beating of her heart. She saw Lance's eyes take note of that stirring cloth as he leaned across her to place the tray on her lap.

"The tea sounds good," she said nervously. "I couldn't have stood anything sweet, but I'm thirsty for something cold."

"Dr. Joshua said you should lay off milk and fruit juice for a few days."

"I never drink milk anyway."

"Never?" he asked.

"No, it's fattening," she answered, taking a bite out of the corner of a piece of toast.

"Ah!" He looked her over carefully, following the outline of her legs under the blankets. "You're a real heavyweight all right." For the first time, she saw a spark of humorous mischief in the depths of his startling blue eyes. He was actually teasing her!

"I might be if I guzzled milk all the time," she said, laughing, and he joined her. "What is this?"

she asked, looking dubiously into the bowl of hot cereal. "It looks like paste."

"I beg your pardon, madam. That bowl of cream of rice is the specialty of the day. There is not one lump in it."

"Cream of rice. Agh!" she shivered. "Do you expect me to *eat* that?"

"Every bite. You need your strength back, and toast alone won't do it. You've got to eat something that will stick to your ribs."

"I think this is going to stick to my throat."

"Now, now, don't insult the chef." He picked up the spoon and ladled a big portion out of the bowl. Stubbornly and without a modicum of compassion, he held it in front of her mouth until she opened it. He shoved the mouthful inside. She had barely swallowed the gooey stuff when he was holding another spoonful for her. She laughed when he began opening and closing his mouth in the way he wanted hers to move.

"This is just like feeding a baby," she managed to say before another bite was pushed into her mouth. "You're very good at it."

"I should be," he said.

God! He's married! she thought. That had never occurred to her. He was probably married and had a house full of children.

"I've been roped into feeding my sister's kids too many times not to have learned a few tricks," he was saying. "That's why I knew about the crackers.

Every time she was pregnant, my sister would go through boxes of soda crackers to control the nausea.''

"Do you have any children of your own?" She had been relieved to hear that he was referring to his nieces and/or nephews, but she still didn't know his marital status. Before she could stop it, the question had popped out. The spoon with the next tasteless lump of cream of rice on it stopped on its journey to her mouth.

"No," he said quietly. "I haven't been married for ten years. The woman I married so ill-advisedly decided after two years of matrimony that I was stifling her and that she wanted a career. She left and filed for divorce." His pragmatic explanation didn't leave much room for discussion, so Erin didn't pursue it. He wasn't married and hadn't been for a long time. For some reason that fact relieved her immensely and made her extremely happy.

After another few bites, she said, "I don't think I want any more. Thank you."

"You've probably had enough for now. For lunch you can have potato soup."

"Vichyssoise?" she asked delightedly.

His light eyebrows lowered in derision and he said flatly, "No, just plain potato soup out of a can." Then they both laughed.

"Tell me about your family," Erin said as Lance removed the tray from her lap. She caught a whiff of shaving soap as he leaned over her. "You have a sister?"

"Yes. She and her husband have four children. When we all get together with Mom and Dad, it's a madhouse."

Erin felt a pang of jealousy. Gerald O'Shea hadn't had any brothers or sisters living. Her mother only had the one sister in Louisiana who was childless and widowed. Erin had hoped she would find Ken with a large family. She longed for relatives. Bloodlines. Descendants. Family.

"I envy you your family," she said. "I always wanted cousins, relatives to visit during the summer and holidays, things like that. I wish Ken and Melanie had children." She sighed. Sometimes the simplest dreams were the most elusive.

Lance crossed the room and stood with his back to her, looking out the window. "We have a lead on Lyman," he said unexpectedly.

She sat up instantly, her lethargy vanishing. "You do? Melanie said last night that she thought you might. What happened?"

"We found out that he rented a car. We had checked out that possibility immediately, of course, but someone missed a private rental firm. When the owner reported to the police that someone had used a phony driver's license, they called us. The man confirmed Lyman's identity when we showed him a picture." He drew a deep breath. "So now we have a concrete lead. We know the kind of car he's driving and the license plate number. We should find him in a matter of days."

There was nothing to say. Erin lay back and

closed her eyes, offering up a silent prayer that her brother would soon come to his senses and turn himself in or at least that he would be found.

"Dr. Joshua sent over a report for you to take back to your doctor in Houston. It's downstairs." Lance didn't sound really interested in the subject and neither was she.

She answered mechanically, "Good. I'll remember to pick it up before I go home."

For the first time Erin noticed that it was raining. Quite hard, in fact. Large round drops were striking the windowpanes, and the eaves of the house were dripping heavily with a haunting percussion. The room was dim, encapsulating, intimate.

"I suppose you'll have to go back to your business and . . . everything . . . after Lyman is found." Lance's voice was low and deep, like the rolling thunder that echoed from hillsides far away. He looked so large outlined against the gray light of the window. His forearm was braced against the window frame. As his head leaned into his fist, his thumb raked back and forth across the cleft in his chin.

"I suppose so," Erin replied vaguely. Suddenly, going back to Houston was a dismal prospect. But she loved her life there! Her business. She was fond of Bart. However, none of that seemed very important any longer. Understanding this man, knowing his needs and meeting them took precedence over everything else. His happiness became essential to hers. Were she forced to choose, at this moment; she would rather be with Lance in this room than anywhere else in the world.

It was almost as if she loved him.

His uncanny knack for reading thoughts didn't fail him. Without moving his body, he turned his head and pierced her with his cerulean eyes.

Her own eyes were wide with the confusion that swept over her. Unaware of what she was doing, she slowly shook her head in denial of the unpredicted emotions coursing through her. Her trembling lips formed his name, but no sound came out. A tear, crowded by the others that were flooding her eyes, slipped over the lower lid and rolled down her pale cheek.

Lance left the window and walked toward the bed. His eyes locked on hers. "Erin?" Her name was barely audible even in the still room.

Then he was beside her, leaning down, supporting himself on still arms spread wide on either side of her. "Erin, why are you crying?" he demanded softly.

"I don't know," she breathed.

"Yes, you do. Why, Erin? Tell me."

She couldn't face him with the knowledge of her love so evident in her eyes. She bowed her head, shaking it again. "I don't know," she said with the barest expulsion of breath.

He lifted her chin with his index finger, forcing her to look at him. "Tell me to go away. Tell me this is insane."

"This is insane," she whispered. Her heart was

thudding. All she could see, wanted to see, was his face only inches from hers.

"Tell me to go away," he grated.

"No," she said, shaking her head in refusal. "I can't."

"Then God help us." The words were scarcely out of his mouth before it was fused with hers.

The mattress sank under his weight as he lay down beside her and gathered her to him. Wasting no time with subtleties, he covered her mouth with his. An insistent tongue pushed past her lips and pillaged the honeyed crevices of her mouth, claiming it as his.

When the initial hunger had been appeased and ownership established, he sipped her slowly. His tongue lifted the remnants of tears off her face, then lingered to taste each feature of her face, her ears, her neck.

She cradled his face between her hands and looked up at him with dark, liquid eyes, swimming with unstemmed, but as yet unshed, tears. "Lance," she luxuriated in saying his name. "Lance, Lance." Raising her head slightly, she kissed the cleft in his chin and aggravated his bottom lip with her teeth until he groaned and pressed her down into the pillows once again, covering her with his body, his mouth fastened onto hers.

Holding her tightly, he rolled them over until Erin was looking down into his face. His hands roamed her back, along her thighs, and over her hips, pressing her ever closer. She adjusted herself over him with a precision so maddening that it forced the breath out of his lungs only to be caught in his throat.

She nibbled at his neck and the triangle at its base was thoroughly explored by a rapacious tongue. Unable to stand any more, he entwined his fingers in her dark hair and raised her mouth to his. Breathless and laughing from sheer joy, he rolled them over onto their sides until they were facing each other. Their heads shared the same pillow. Fingers traced; noses nuzzled; mouths nibbled. They relished each other.

Timidly, Erin raised her hands to the necktie knotted below his top shirt button. With awkward fingers, she loosed it until she could ease it over his head. He accommodated her by raising his head off the pillow. He could be patient with her blunderings. He had all the time in the world.

Her fingers worked with the buttons on his shirt until they were all undone. Then she pushed the smooth cotton aside. She studied him for a moment. He was so boldly virile that she knew a moment of shyness. "I think you're beautifully made, Lance," she said unevenly.

Still timid, but tempted beyond endurance, she placed her hands on him and combed through the thick mat of tawny hair on his chest with her fingers.

"You have a gray hair!" she exclaimed. "Right here," she said, tweaking the novelty.

"Ouch! That's attached, you know."

"How old are you?" she asked, soothingly rubbing the spot where she had pulled the hair.

"Thirty-seven."

"I thought you were thirty-three. But that's when I thought you were Ken."

"Nope. I'm an old man. Much too old for you." His fingers were memorizing her collarbone.

"I've always had a penchant for antiques," she teased, as her hands smoothed over the hard muscles beneath the furred skin.

He indulged her idle, playful exploration until she touched his nipples with inquisitive fingers. His breath hissed out from between his lips and he caught her hands and pressed them over the hard, distended buds.

"You're not playing fair," he scolded her tenderly and kissed her briefly on the mouth.

"Teach me the rules," she taunted softly.

He raised her hands and wrapped her arms around his neck. The twelve tiny pearl buttons that formed a neat row from the yoke of her nightgown to her waist taxed his patience. But when he was finished, he paused for a moment, savoring the anticipation before he separated the folds of wispy fabric.

His eyes wandered leisurely over her, and Erin wondered at her own immodesty. Even when his fingers followed the path his eyes had charted, she could conjure up no inhibitions.

Gently he cupped her breasts in his hands and lifted them slightly. Heavy lids screened her eyes as his thumbs stroked her until she felt herself tauten under this bewitching manipulation.

"You're beautiful," he sighed. "Just as I knew you were. Just as I *felt* you were."

Her throat hurt with the constricted muscles unable to contain her emotion. Her fingers outlined his lips as she entreated him, "Please," and drew his head down to her.

His mouth was wet and hot as he closed it over the rose-tinted crest. He tugged on her gently, then tortured her with his flicking tongue. His hand was at the small of her back, urging her hips against the hard tension in his. When she moved so eagerly and naturally against him, a deep moan issued out of his throat and in desperation he clasped her to him.

He heard that now familiar purring in her throat that made the blood pound in his veins. That sound, her scent, the feel and taste of her, filled his brain and obliterated every rational, reasonable, responsible thought. Even as he argued with himself that this was lunacy, he was helplessly drowning in the essence of Erin O'Shea.

He left the bed only long enough to strip off his clothes. Erin studied him and experienced no fearful dread even when his aroused virility was fully revealed. Carefully he sat down on the bed and eased the nightgown off her shoulders and down her body. His eyes were hungry and devoured every inch of her before he lay down, blanketing her body with his.

They had both come home.

Their breaths mingled and spiraled above them as they each released a long, contented sigh. Lance buried his face between her breasts and held her tightly. Erin's arms wound around his back. His naked masculinity so complemented her femininity that they both gloried in the contrasts—hair-roughened skin against silkiness, hard muscle against soft curve, throbbing power against a welcoming vulnerability.

His hands began a sensuous assault, thrilling her with every touch. They found her breasts and massaged them gently, then grew bolder and teased the responsive nipples into hardness. Lowering his head, he took her nipple between his lips and laved it with his tongue until she heard soft cries of bliss and realized that they had come from her own lips.

Murmuring his name, Erin arched and writhed along his large body, but he held her away from him by placing his hand on her stomach, his thumb between her ribs. He started a slow, mesmerizing descent. How could a hand, fingers, a thumb possess such provocative powers? Yet when they continued downward to discover the secrets of her body, it was she who gasped at the revelations.

Without persuasion, she countenanced a more thorough exploration. Sweetly he tormented her. His fingers deftly separated the protective petals and tenderly stroked that center of her desire that was moist and yielding. "Erin," was all he said, but the wonder in his voice conveyed a million unspoken meanings.

Arching against him, she cried his name. Or was it merely an echo that reverberated in her brain? Hearing her plea, whether vocal or silent, he greeted it with an obliging thrust.

Then he became perfectly still and looked down into her eyes with disbelief.

"My God, Erin. Why didn't you tell me?" he asked in a soft, urgent whisper.

"I didn't think it was important," she answered in kind.

He searched her eyes with his. "You're wrong. It's very important."

"I don't mean to minimize its importance. It's just that right now it doesn't matter."

"What does matter?"

She touched his face with trembling fingers. "Being good for you."

"Oh God," he breathed as he kissed her and broke that last seal of her innocence.

They moved together as though choreographed, in perfect synchronization, each bringing the other to the height of ecstasy and filling a need that hadn't even been realized until now.

There was no explanation for this spontaneous act of love. Had they taken the time to examine their motivations, they couldn't have found a logical reason for it. They were victims of an ancient force that made no apology or justification for its being. It didn't even exist until it was born between two people. And that was justification enough.

Patiently whispering words, the meanings of

which were unintelligible and unimportant, Lance encouraged her, bringing her to a destiny she couldn't have anticipated. When she reached it, he joined her on the crest of the wave, and she felt his full magnificence fill a void deep inside her.

He didn't leave her immediately. His breathing was harsh and uneven in her ear as he nuzzled it with his feverish face. He held her tenderly, but possessively. Did he think she was a mirage? The stroking hands that celebrated her body seemed to fear that she would evaporate at any moment.

When she adjusted her hips more comfortably under his weight, he made a moaning sound that diminished into a shuddering sigh of delight. An answering passion championed her original dismay when he began to move inside her again.

Finally when they were totally spent and their breathing had returned to normal, he left that warm, silken harbor. With their legs entwined, he pulled her close and nestled her head against his chest.

"Are you okay?" he asked. His fingers traveled up and down her spine.

"Slightly better than okay," she said.

A deep chuckle rumbled in her ear and she raised her head. "You're laughing," she said in surprise.

"Is that so unusual?" He quirked an eyebrow quizzically.

"For you it is. You rarely smile, you know," she chided gently.

He smiled then, but his eyes were serious. "You make me smile," he whispered.

"Do I?"

"Yes. You do." He kissed her deeply. When her tongue darted past his and sought the interior of his mouth, he pushed away from her. "Erin, stop that or I won't be able to. And you're supposed to be sick." He got up from the bed and began to dress. "What kind of a cad do you take me for, to insinuate myself on a helpless, weak woman? Besides all that, I'm on duty. Government business." His grin was decidedly wicked. "But this has been one helluva coffee break."

Erin giggled. "You're improving. You even made a joke."

He pulled on a pair of brief blue underwear. She sighed in the pleasure of watching him dress. "Somehow you never struck me as the type to wear such sexy underwear. You look almost as good in it as you do out of it," she said impishly.

He cast a look at her that was mockingly stern. Then he broke into a wide smile. "I bet you say that to all the boys," he said coyly. She laughed again.

When he was dressed, he came back to the bed and leaned over her. "Are you really all right? I didn't intend to be so greedy, but, Erin, you . . ." He couldn't finish without kissing her again. "Did I hurt you?" There was no mistaking the concern in his voice.

"Yes, Lance, I'm all right. And no, you didn't hurt me any more than I wanted to be hurt." She smiled lovingly as she brushed back errant strands of hair from his forehead. "It was beautiful and I'm wonderful."

He sat down on the edge of the bed and took both her hands in his. "Erin," he said slowly. His thumb was drawing a circle in her palm and he stared at it fixedly. Then he lifted his eyes to meet hers. "There are so many unanswered questions, but I didn't want to talk about other men when I was in bed with you."

"No. I understand."

He bent over her and kissed her once on the soft curve of her breast, then tenderly on her mouth. "Can I see you later?" he asked, raking her with his eyes and lending a double meaning to his words.

"Um-hum," she said lazily. It was a promise.

"Get some rest." He kissed her lightly on the forehead and left the room.

CHAPTER
Eight

Several hours later she was coming out of the bathroom rubbing her wet hair with a towel when someone knocked on the bedroom door. She was securely wrapped in a terrycloth robe, so she said, "Come in."

Mike stuck his head around the opened door. "Miss O'Shea, you have a call from Bart something or other. Do you want to take it?"

Bart! In startled reaction she pressed her fingers against compressed lips. Mike looked at her curiously and she stammered, "Y—yes, I'll take it. Ask him to wait a moment, please."

"Just pick up the telephone in Mrs. Lyman's room and you won't have to come downstairs."

"Thank you, Mike."

He was almost out the door when he turned around and said, "By the way, I'm glad you're feeling better." Before she had time to respond, he had ducked his head shyly and scooted out the door. Compared to Mike's usual terseness, the speech was elocutionary.

Erin returned the damp towel to the bathroom and mercilessly raked a comb through her wet curls. She was buying time. What could she say to Bart? She didn't want to talk to him so soon after having made love to Lance.

She'd fallen asleep after he left her and hadn't had time to properly cherish her reactions to their shared intimacy. The enormity of what had happened was still too new, too private, too sacred. She wanted to ponder this momentous occasion, restructure the scene, relive each sensation, listen as her mind played back each stirring word Lance had said.

But if she didn't talk to Bart, no telling what he might do. He might jump to a wrong—or right—conclusion and do something impulsive.

She sighed as she left her room and went into Melanie's. It would be better to talk to him now rather than later. Long distance was no way to break an engagement, so she would talk to him normally. As soon as she was able to return to Houston, she would have to tell him she couldn't marry him.

Especially now.

"Hello," Erin said into the receiver.

"Well it's about time, sugar. What in the hell took so long? I've been hangin' on this damn phone for five minutes. You okay, baby?"

Had Bart ever called her by name? she thought crossly. She was instantly sorry for her vexation and said as cheerfully as she could, "I'm fine, Bart. I'm sorry for the delay." She offered no explanation for it.

"How's your brother? Do you like him?" Bart's voice grated on her. His heartiness and constant good humor seemed trite somehow. So unlike a man who felt things deeply, took things seriously, and when he did laugh, it was very special. "Sugar, are you asleep?" Bart boomed into the receiver.

"Oh, no. I . . . uh . . . I haven't exactly met Ken yet," she demurred.

"How come, baby? Nothing's wrong, is it?"

"No, no," she hastened to say. "It's just that he's out of town on business and his wife, Melanie, whom I adore, thought it would be best if we didn't tell him anything until he . . . uh . . . finished this business deal he's involved in." Did that sound plausible? She wasn't accustomed to lying and it didn't come easy to her. It was so hard to concentrate. She kept seeing Lance's impassioned face hovering over hers and hearing those precious love words he had chanted gruffly in her ear.

"I just got back from the Panhandle yesterday. We brought in another well, sugar. Sure wish you'd been here to celebrate with me."

"That's wonderful, Bart," she said. What difference did another well make? He had about thirty others.

"I called your office first thing this morning and Betty gave me this number. Who was the guy that answered if it wasn't your brother?"

Never underestimate Bart's cunning. "That . . ." Think, Erin! "That was a business associate of Ken's. He had stopped by to leave some papers. Melanie and I were out in the flower garden. That's what took so long to answer the telephone. He had to find us."

She didn't want to tell him about her illness. It would be just like him to catch the next plane to San Francisco. Last fall she had contracted a common cold. The next morning she had dragged herself out of bed to answer the doorbell and was astounded to find a registered nurse standing on her porch reporting for duty. Bart had insisted. No, she didn't want him to know she had been sick.

"When is that brother of yours coming back? When are you coming home? I'm as lonesome as a polecat, honey. I miss you."

What was it Lance had rasped in her ear? "Lift . . . ah, Erin . . . Yes, that's it . . . Yes . . . I'll wait . . . I'll wait darling . . . but hurry!" "I miss you, too, Bart," she heard herself say without consciously thinking the words.

"I know this is important to you, darlin', or I wouldn't sit still for you being gone so long."

"And I know that you're not nearly as lonely as you're making it sound," she said lightly. "Have you cut down your dinner parties from six to four this week?"

"Now, come on, honey. Don't tease me," Bart whined. "You know I don't enjoy anything unless you're there with me. Hurry on home, sweetheart. I love you, you know."

Erin swallowed hard. Had Lance mentioned love? Had she? Had she said, "Lance, I love you"? She didn't think so. She would have remembered. "I know you do, Bart," she whispered. "And I love you." Only not *that* way. Not enough. Not nearly enough. Not like—

"Do you need anything? Money? Can I do something for you here?"

He really was terribly kind to her. Would he be hurt when she told him she had fallen suddenly, but irrevocably, in love with another man? "No, Bart. I'm fine. I'll call you in a day or two and let you know my plans."

"Okay, honey. You take care now. There are some real weird dudes in San Francisco, you know. Be careful."

"I will. I promise. Good-bye, Bart."

"Bye-bye, baby."

Erin looked down at the diamond on her finger and admired it for what it was—a priceless, flawless gem. But its reflection was cold. It radiated no warmth. It didn't touch her heart with fire the way a pair of blue eyes under golden eyebrows did. Those eyes had more facets and capricious prisms of light than did the perfectly cut stone.

She slipped the ring from her finger and, having walked somnambulantly back into the guest bedroom, went to the dressing table where she had left her travel jewelry case. Lifting the lid, she dropped the ring inside and closed the box with a decisive snap.

By the time she had dried and styled her hair and dressed in a casual pair of wool slacks and an angora sweater, she was trembling with weakness. The hot steamy bath she had taken had felt wonderful, but it had left her weak and light-headed. She desperately needed sustenance.

She went downstairs and spoke to Mike, who was sitting within reach of the telephone on the living room desk. Going into the kitchen, she switched on the light. The rain had stopped, but the afternoon was still cloudy and dark. She couldn't find the can of potato soup that Lance had referred to, so she fixed herself a grilled cheese sandwich and a cup of bouillon.

Nearly all the sandwich was gone, and she sat sipping the broth when the back door opened and Lance came in. Her face brightened immediately. She knew she looked fresh and pretty, flushing with the anticipation of their seeing each other again. Would he dare kiss her with Mike so near?

A happy hello froze on her lips and was never uttered when Lance turned around after closing the door and faced her. His features were harder and colder than they had been that first day when he had answered the doorbell. His eyes glinted like chips of blue ice as they pierced through her. His body was tense, the muscles bunched in anger.

"I see you're feeling stronger. It's amazing what a little exercise can do." His tone was bitter and the words were harsh, deliberately hurtful, and full of innuendo.

"I'm much better," she said apprehensively. Why was he glaring at her like that? "W—would you like something?" She hated herself for stammering. What had she done that was so offensive? Didn't he remember what had happened just a few hours ago?

"No. I hate bouillon."

"Something cold?"

"No, thank you, Miss O'Shea," he said with exaggerated politeness. "Actually I came to see if you'd lend me your car. Your rental car," he corrected. "Clark just called and the car he took Mrs. Lyman in has broken down. They're stranded at a garage. She asked if I would come pick her up."

"Yes, certainly."

"She asked that you come with me—if you feel up to it."

Erin stood up shakily and nodded. "I'll be glad to go. I could use some fresh air."

"I don't know why, Miss O'Shea. You seem in perfect physical condition to me," he sneered. He turned his back on her and left the room, going toward the living room.

Why was he acting this way? What had happened in the space of a few hours to convert the tender, fierce lover into this sarcastic, hateful man? How could he, anyone, deride such an explosive sexual union?

The answer to her own question hit her like a bucket of cold water in the face. It hadn't been that earthshaking to him. Affairs like that were probably commonplace to a man like Lance. In this instance love wasn't blind. She knew other women would be just as attracted to his virile good looks as she was. Erin O'Shea would join the ranks of women who had temporarily sated Lance Barrett's sexual appetite. He could easily forget what had happened.

She had been the oldest kind of fool. Not one word of coy protest had she uttered. Her conscience had failed her completely. Erin O'Shea, who had always prided herself on her upright morality and circumspect life-style, had given her body to a man without one consideration of the moral consequences. Now, because of Lance's attitude, she was deluged with guilt and self-deprecation.

He could treat her with inexcusable rudeness and scorn and then blithely turn his back on her and saunter out of the room. Had he screamed abusive insults at her, she could have withstood them, for she felt they were well deserved. But suddenly she was extremely angry. Like most women, the one thing Erin couldn't tolerate from a man was indifference.

She flew out of the kitchen, her eyes stormy, ready to do battle. She lost her impetus when she saw him leaning over the desk talking calmly to Mike. He was wearing his glasses as he studied a report one of his agents had called in. Just then he reached up and shoved them to the top of his forehead. It was such an endearing habit. *Lance, what's wrong?* she cried silently.

He wheeled toward her as if he had heard her words. *Dammit!* he cursed to himself. Why did she have to look so beautiful? The coral sweater enhanced the creaminess of her complexion that he knew extended all over her body. The gray slacks fit her tidy little fanny like a glove and he could almost feel those firm muscles in his palms. The dark, soft curls fell gently around her head and he knew how they could curl sensuously around a man's fingers. Her eyes, which had bewitched him from the first time he had looked into them, now radiated a glow. A glow that unmistakably bespoke recent knowledge of a man. Him.

He had almost convinced himself that when he saw her again, away from the rain-induced ambience of the bedroom, the mystery of it all would be revealed as a sham, the magic would be exposed as a hoax. Nothing could have been that good. His deceiving brain had magnified a minor sexual experiment into a soul-rending experience.

How could she have lived this long, looking like she did, and never have had a man? His unexpected enlightenment on her virginity had almost stopped him. Almost. At that point, hell or high water couldn't have stopped him.

But what about her husband? Maybe she *had* been lying about that. That fancy fiancé of hers must be the dumbest bastard in the world. Anybody stupid enough to let a woman like that remain innocent deserved to be betrayed by the scheming little bitch.

He drew an inward sigh. *All right, Barrett, she isn't a scheming bitch*. Until a few hours ago, she had been a virgin. Lance Barrett had never been a despoiler of virgins. He hadn't forced her. Why had she submitted without a word?

Why? Why had she let him make love to her? Beyond that, why had she participated to the point of making him feel like, until this morning, he had been a virgin too?

Never had he been accepted so deeply and unrestrainedly. She had entrapped him with such tight perfection that it had transcended mere physical union and encompassed spiritual absorption. Even after he had given her all of himself, he had been reluctant to forsake the intimacy that bound his body to hers. Only an act of will had enabled him to leave her before he became a victim of that driving hunger again.

Now he looked at her and didn't know whether to slap her hard across her lying mouth or kiss it until she cried out his name as she had when a blinding light had exploded in them simultaneously and forged them together.

Brusquely he said, "Get your coat and the car keys." Turning to Mike he said, "This shouldn't take long. I'll be back shortly."

"Sure, Lance," was Mike's only reply.

His hand, wrapped around her upper arm, was

firm as he ushered her out the door and toward the Mercedes. "Do you trust me to drive?" he asked.

"The only thing I can trust you to do is behave like a barbarian." She jerked her arm away and flung the keys at him. She went around to the passenger side unescorted. Both doors were slammed jarringly and he started the motor, cursing under his breath when the cold engine took its time to warm up. Finally he shoved the car into gear and they lurched out of the driveway.

It was good to be outside. Erin pressed the button that automatically lowered her window and breathed in the frosty evening air. They sped along the streets in silence. Lance's hands were firm on the wheel and he never took his eyes off the road.

Puzzlement, hurt, and anger vied for supremacy in Erin's mind, but she refused to allow Lance to see how upset she was. It would be a cold day in hell before she would ask what had happened that so drastically changed his mind about her. She didn't have to wait long before she found out.

Erin looked at him in surprise as he whipped the car off the main thoroughfare and wended through tree-lined lanes. She realized that they were in Golden Gate Park, but this particular area was unlit and deserted. He braked the car sharply and cut the engine. Large trees spread naked limbs over them like an umbrella bereft of its silk. The foggy mist of evening swathed them in heavy silence.

Lance lay his right arm along the back of the seat as he faced her. Deep shadows were cast on the planes and hollows of his face, making him appear sinister. Erin felt a momentary prickle of fear.

"You must be very proud of yourself, Miss O'Shea."

"What do you mean?" she asked.

"I mean that you have made a prize jackass out of a man old enough to know better."

"Please, Lance, I don't know what you mean." She strove to be reasonable over the pounding of her pulse. "Shouldn't we be meeting—"

"They can wait," he snapped. "I want to have this out with you here and now."

Her own anger was growing under the condescending tone in his voice. "Have what out with me? I don't know what you're talking about."

To her amazement, he grinned, but the smile never reached his eyes. "You sure are being missed by that lonesome ol' polecat, sugar," he said in a perfect imitation of Bart's Texas twang.

Comprehension dawned on her and she was suffused with mortification and fury. "You listened! You eavesdropped on my conversation!"

He shrugged negligently. "Habit. I listen to all the calls coming into the Lymans' house. You knew that."

She did, but she had forgotten. "But you knew that that particular call was for me personally. It couldn't have been of any interest to you!"

"Oh, but it was, Miss O'Shea," he objected smoothly. "You'd be amazed at how informative I found it to be. Now I know what a two-timing little liar you are."

"I am not!" she denied heatedly.

"No? 'I miss you, Bart. I love you, Bart,' " he mimicked. "You failed to mention to good ol' Bart what you were doing just before he called."

"That's disgusting," she spat.

"You're damn right it is," he shouted. "I think Bart would find it quite disgusting to learn that this morning his fiancée was learning to screw with unequaled aptitude."

She didn't think before she slapped him. She hadn't even realized that she had until the sound cracked through the tense atmosphere of the car. Her palm stung, but it was worth the pain to see the stunned expression on Lance's face. Her victory was short-lived, however, because he was galvanized into action. Reaching across the car, he grabbed her wrist in an iron grip.

"If you ever do that again, I'll break your arm," he threatened and she believed him. His voice sounded like he had gravel in his throat. "I know your type, Miss O'Shea."

She winced under the pressure of his fingers on her wrist. "I'm not a type," she argued with more spirit than she felt.

"Yes, you are," he said with deceptive softness. "It's fun to have a lark with the government agent, play spy games, but you know you have your Texas millionaire to go home to."

"No," she said. Tears of pain were streaming down her cheeks. Not physical pain from his fingers digging into her flesh, but pain from realizing the low opinion he had of her. If only he'd let her explain.

"Well, the game is over. You may enjoy slumming it with me, but I never play out of my league."

"League?" she asked remorsefully. "Why do you think we're in different leagues?"

"Because, dammit, you drive a white Mercedes and I drive a maroon Chevette. Doesn't that tell you anything?" He released her wrist so abruptly that she was staggered and bumped against him in inertia. He moved away from her and stared out the opposite window.

It took several moments for his meaning to sink in. When it did, she bristled with fury. "How dare you insult me like that!" she gasped. "How dare you think it would matter to me what kind of car a man drives or how much money he has. I . . . I slept . . . slept with you because I wanted to."

"Did you?" he asked silkily, facing her once again. He lunged toward her, pinning her against the back of the seat with his hands on her shoulders. He leaned into her. "Don't you like the way Stanton makes love? What excuse were you going to give poor ol' Bart on your wedding night when he found you less than pure? But then he'll naturally assume that your husband took what by right should belong to him."

"Stop it, please," she sobbed.

He settled on her heavily and whispered degradingly, "When he holds you, do you mold to him like this?" She wriggled and tried to push him away, but he was too strong and the movement of his body against hers made his point for him. "When he kisses you, do you make that purring sound in your throat?"

He tried to kiss her, but she twisted her head away from him. His hand grasped her jaw and held her head immobile as his lips crushed hers brutally. She fought him, but his hold on her was unyielding. The pressure of his fingers on her jaw was so strong that she feared any moment the cracking of her bones.

"Does your body respond to him the way it does to me?"

He flung aside her coat and covered her breast with his hand. In opposition to her will, she could feel herself responding to his touch. His fingers pressed into the soft mound of flesh and then began to stroke her. What had been intended as an assault became a caress. He slipped his hand under her sweater and squeezed her until her flesh was crowded between his fingers. He unclasped her bra and captured a taut nipple with fingers no longer cruel, but dedicated to giving pleasure.

Only his mouth continued its onslaught. And gradually it, too, ceased to plunder and began to persuade. The kiss changed character so subtly that Erin wasn't even aware of it until she heard herself moaning in acquiescence. Her lips softened and accepted the alluring power of his tongue. Her body became pliant under his exploring hands. She wasn't even aware of saying, "Oh, Lance," until he yanked himself away from her.

His name, recited in his ear with such disillusionment, penetrated that wall of anger and resentment he had erected since hearing her conversation with Stanton. He retreated swiftly behind the steering wheel of the car and gripped it with his hands as if to pull it away and destroy it. He rested his forehead on the backs of his hands.

God! What had he almost done?!

Erin watched with a feeling of empty helplessness. Lance's shoulders slumped, and the heels of his hands were digging into his eye sockets while his fingers made deep furrows in the thick, mussed, sun-gilded hair. His chest was heaving as he gasped for restorative breath.

Finally, he raised supplicant eyes to her and opened his arms in a gesture of bewilderment. "I'm sorry," he said. "Never, *never* in my life have I . . . If I've hurt you . . . I'm sorry," he repeated hoarsely. He squeezed his eyes shut and pinched the bridge of his nose with his thumb and index finger. He spoke more to himself than to her in a voice full of desperation. "I don't know what's happening to me."

Melanie seemed unaware of and indifferent to the tension between the other two passengers of the car The three of them rode home in remote silence.

Erin had noted that her sister-in-law's eyes were red and puffy, testifying that she had been crying recently. The usually effervescent woman had barely mumbled a hello to her and Lance when they pulled into the garage and she had climbed into the backseat. Lance had instructed Clark to stay with the car until the minor repair was made.

Melanie huddled in the corner of the backseat and made it apparent that she wasn't in a mood to talk. Since her arrival in San Francisco, Erin didn't remember seeing Melanie quite this despondent. It was a depression too deep for tears, a hopeless despair that finds no release through normal channels.

As soon as they walked through the front door of her house, Melanie apologized, but excused herself and ascended the stairs.

Not a word was exchanged between Lance and Erin. She hung her coat on the hall tree and proceeded into the kitchen to get a drink of water. When she walked back through the hallway toward the stairs, she met Lance as he was coming out of the living room after consulting with Mike.

The cold, impersonal nod he gave her was like that of a stranger. Only today she had been lying in his arms, listening to an outpouring of passion. She knew his body intimately, yet she knew the man not at all. His anger had been explained. He had overheard her conversation with Bart and totally misconstrued it.

How could he think her capable of such duplicity? Did he truly think that she could take what had happened between them so casually? If he did, he didn't know her. Which was precisely the point. They didn't know each other in the ways that were important.

Once she got to her room, it didn't take her long to prepare for bed. She had just snapped out the light in the bathroom and was crossing to the bed when there was a timid knock on her door.

"It's me."

"Come in, Melanie. I'm not in bed yet," Erin answered.

Melanie came in dressed for bed with a light robe covering her nightgown. "Am I disturbing you?"

"Of course not."

"How was your day?" Erin asked the younger woman who collapsed dispiritedly into the armchair.

"It was terrible, Erin." The blond head shook from side to side. She twisted the wedding ring on her finger. "My parents drive me crazy. They called early this morning, insisting that I come visit them today. Do you know what they wanted to see me about? Divorce. They want me to file for a divorce from Ken."

"Oh, Melanie! How could they even suggest such a thing at a time like this?"

"I don't know. I wouldn't even listen, of course, but they kept on giving me all the reasons I should. They don't honor the one reason that I wouldn't. I love Ken." She buried her face in her hands and began to cry with wracking sobs that tore Erin's heart in two. She knelt down in front of her sister-in-law and drew her into comforting arms.

"It's Father's fault that Ken did what he did anyway. He was always pressuring Ken, giving him impossible tasks at the bank and then embarrassing him in front of other people when he couldn't carry them out. Ken tried very hard, but his best was never good enough. For the past year or so, he wanted to change jobs, but I begged him not to. Father didn't have any sons, you see, and I thought that Ken might be able to fill that gap that I couldn't. I was so selfish. I didn't see what all of this was doing to Ken as a man."

"Don't blame yourself, Melanie. Ken is an adult. He may have been hurting inside and feeling insufficient and insecure, but he's done something wrong and he'll have to pay the consequences. He realizes that. He doesn't blame you, I'm sure."

"Then why hasn't he even tried to contact me? I haven't seen or heard from him since he left for work that morning. Erin, I'm miserable without him."

Erin sighed and patted Melanie on the back, providing what small amount of solace she could. "I think he doesn't contact you because he loves you. He doesn't want you to become involved. He's protecting you."

"I could use less protection and more of him."

Erin smiled gently. "I can understand that, but I

doubt if a man could.'' Her thoughts turned introspective for a moment and she said, ''They see things so differently than we do.''

Melanie blew her nose on a tissue Erin handed her. Wiping the tears out of her eyes, she said, ''I haven't been around to help you today. I haven't even asked how you felt.''

''I'm fine. Much better.''

Melanie nodded absently. Erin could see that she was still distraught. Her husband's absence was causing her anguish, anguish she must suffer alone.

Confirming Erin's surmise, Melanie said, ''If you don't mind, I think I'll go back to my room. I'm not very good company tonight. I want to lie in the bed I share with Ken and think about him. Does that sound crazy?''

''It sounds perfectly normal. If you need to talk to someone in the middle of the night, I'm available. You won't be disturbing me.''

''Thanks, Erin. I . . . I'm really glad you're here.''

Thin arms went around Erin's neck and she hugged Melanie closer. ''I'm glad I'm here, too. Good night.''

''Good night.''

Erin had slept so much during the day that she didn't think she would be able to fall asleep, but it was amazingly simple. She wanted to analyze Lance's peculiar behavior, but her brain refused to focus on that. Ken's disappearance was a problem she still had to cope with, and Melanie's unhappiness troubled her as well. Defensively, her brain shut out these burdensome thoughts and she fell asleep the moment she lay her head on the pillow.

Her dreams were full of Lance. One moment he was cruel and vindictive. The next, she was locked in an intoxicating embrace and he was making love to her. Her fingertips could feel the texture of his hair where it lay against his neck. His scent was so familiar to her now, she was engulfed in it as he moved against her. He was repeating her name close to her ear. Erin, Erin, Erin. She drew him closer still and clasped her hands behind his neck.

For a moment, after she opened her eyes, she thought she was in an extension of her dream. Lance was saying her name softly. He leaned over her. Her arms were tight around his neck.

"What—" she gasped, pulling her arms back and reaching hastily for the covers.

CHAPTER

Nine

"Shhhh, it's okay. I'm sorry if I scared you," he whispered. "Erin—"

"What are you doing here?" she demanded angrily. What kind of game was he playing now? She didn't trust him. He was too unpredictable. She didn't understand him. Nor did she understand why her heart was pounding and her body trembling as though the dream had been real. It had been so vivid. She could feel—

"Erin, I have something to tell you. Do you want me to turn on the light?" She shook her head no. "We've had some news. It's not good. I need you to help me tell Mrs. Lyman."

"Ken?"

She could see his head nodding before he said, "Yes." A foreboding cloaked her with dread.

"Oh, God," she whimpered. "Lance, you found him?"

"Yes." He took a deep breath. In the darkness he found her clenched hands being pressed against her lips. He took them in his hand and warmed them between strong fingers. "Erin, he's dead."

"No," she breathed, shaking her head in denial. It couldn't be true. God wasn't that cruel. "No," she said aloud with more emphasis.

Lance took her by the shoulders and said, "I'm sorry, Erin, believe me. They found him late last night in a dumpy hotel room on the outskirts of San Diego. Apparently he was waiting to slip across the border."

She was trying to absorb all the facts, but couldn't. Only one grim truth had significance. She would never see her brother alive. Kenneth Lyman was dead. She realized that Lance had stopped talking and asked listlessly, "How?" Did it matter?

"We'll go into that later—"

"Tell me now," she said levelly.

"He was murdered," Lance sighed. "He had been robbed of pocket money, his watch, things like that. Ironically, the suitcase with all the money in it was found intact under his bed." He waited for a moment before asking, "Are you all right?"

"Yes," she said. Her calmness surprised her. "We'd better go tell Melanie." She didn't wait for him to say anything. She got out of bed and slipped into a robe. When she turned around, he was already out in the hallway.

At the door of Melanie's room he suggested,

"Why don't you go in and wake her up. Call me when you're ready."

It was the hardest thing she had ever had to do in her life, but Erin went into the room, awakened Melanie, helped her get into her robe, and then stood by while Lance told the young woman about her husband's death. Erin would have expected her sister-in-law to faint, cry, scream, or go into hysterics. But she listened calmly and dry-eyed.

When Lance finally finished telling her the facts, sparing her the details, she said tonelessly, "I think I knew that he was dead. I've had a feeling all day that I'd never see him again. It's strange how I knew."

She asked Lance what procedure they must follow and he answered her. "Well, we're sure it's him, but unfortunately you'll have to go down there and identify the body. Because his demise was the result of a crime, you'll have to sign a lot of papers to have the body released. I can help you with all of that."

"Thank you, Mr. Barrett. I'll need your help, I'm sure."

"I'll call your parents—"

"No!" Melanie said with a newly acquired maturity. "I'll do this myself. Except I want Erin to come with me."

Lance looked as if he were about to object on that point, but Erin said, "Of course," before he had a chance to speak.

His face showed grim acceptance as he checked his wristwatch and said, "I'll make the airline reservations. It's six thirty now. Can you be ready in two hours or so?"

"Yes, we'll be ready," Melanie stated calmly.

The events of the next day and a half were forever a conglomeration of hazy recollections for Erin. She couldn't remember everything, though certain incidents would remain in her mind for the rest of her life.

Somehow she and Melanie managed to get themselves ready for the trip to San Diego in the allotted amount of time. They dressed for comfort and efficiency. Erin wore a navy blazer over an ivory silk blouse. Her skirt was caramel-colored wool. As they left the house, she took her leather trench coat off the halltree and carried it over her arm.

Melanie was similarly dressed and had pulled her hair back into a severe ponytail. Her face looked naked, scrubbed clean of makeup. But she was beautiful in the way of tragic heroines. Erin's heart went out to the young woman who exhibited such courage.

Lance drove the repaired government car to the airport. Melanie sat quietly in her corner of the backseat. Erin's eyes were brimming with tears, but Melanie's remained dry. Her only evidence of grief was to grip Erin's hand during the flight from San Francisco to San Diego. They sat on the window and aisle seats, placing their purses and coats in the

seat between them. Lance sat across the aisle from
them and stared out the window for the entire trip.
He was polite to Melanie. He showed the same
courtesy to Erin, but it was impersonal and remote.

When they were met at the airport by a man
of Mike's caliber, he ushered them to yet another
innocuous automobile. Lance sat in the front seat
next to the taciturn driver while Erin and Melanie
shared the backseat. The two men conversed in low
tones, but their exact words were indistinct. Melanie
watched the traffic and passing landscape like one
hypnotized.

For hours it seemed they alternately stood or sat
in dim, hushed corridors waiting for one official or
another. Lance was in and out of offices, conferring
with soberly dressed men who looked curiously at
Melanie. Every so often she was interrogated. She
answered the questions listlessly, but honestly.

Erin was rarely spoken to. Her only responsibility
was to provide support to Melanie, who was going
through this ordeal with more aplomb than Erin
would ever have guessed she possessed.

Thankfully, Erin had to concede that Lance
shielded Melanie from many of the unpleasantries.
He must have cut through miles of red tape and
helped to expedite the endless legal procedures. Every law enforcement agency—federal, state, and
local—seemed to be involved to some extent, and
each had to be provided with information and answers.

The sun had long since set when they left the

last of the austere offices and drove to the county hospital. Erin dreaded this last stop. Although his identity had already been confirmed, they must go to the morgue and look at Ken's body before it could be released to them.

The man who had met them at the airport was escorting Melanie down the hallway toward a forbidding door at its end. Erin was following them. Lance was behind her.

Before they reached that looming door, he grasped her upper arm and turned her around to face him. "Erin, you're not going in there," he said quietly but firmly.

"Yes, I am. Melanie needs me."

"I'm going with her. You're not going in there," he repeated.

"Don't tell me what I am or am not going to do." She pulled her arm free of his firm grip. "I want to see my brother."

"No, you don't. Not like that." He took both her arms then. "Think, Erin. You have an image of him. He was a healthy, good-looking young man. Wouldn't you rather always think of him that way as . . ." His voice trailed off. Then he urged, "You don't want your only vision of him to be like he is now. Don't go in there."

His pleading eyes and the tense, anxious set of his mouth convinced her he was right. She nodded her assent and slumped against him in defeat. He led her to a vinyl-covered sofa and sat her down.

The other two had reached the door to the morgue and were waiting expectantly for Lance. He settled a reassuring hand on Erin's shoulder and whispered, "I won't be but a minute."

When the trio came back out into the hallway, Melanie was crying softly into a man's handkerchief. Erin rushed toward her and put her arms around the younger woman who seemed to have shrunk in the last few minutes.

In her hand she clutched a white piece of paper. Her tear-streaked face was pitiful as she looked at Erin. "They found this in his pocket. It's a letter to me, Erin. He loved me. He says so. He loved me." She fell against Erin's declining strength and sobbed as she continued to aver Ken's love for her.

Erin held Melanie against her as they sat on the same uncomfortable sofa while Lance arranged for the transport of Ken's body to San Francisco. Erin was glad that Melanie was crying. It was a much needed release and tears were cleansing. A weeping griever was better than the zombie Melanie had been all day, merely performing as she was expected to.

During the drive back to the airport and while they awaited their flight, Melanie continued to vent her grief. She was exhausted by the time they boarded the airplane. Luckily the late-night flight wasn't crowded.

A sensitive, sympathetic flight attendant suggested that they remove the arms separating the individual seats and allow Melanie to lie down. She

didn't argue, and by the time Erin covered her with
a blanket, she was subdued and lying with her tear-
swollen eyes closed.

Lance, who had been conferring with his associate, was the last passenger to board. He took a seat
beside Erin, stowing an ordinary looking suitcase
under the seat in front of him. Erin knew what it
must be and averted her eyes from it. The brown
suitcase was something hideous that had destroyed
her brother's life.

After the plane had taken off into the darkness
and the lights of San Diego had become no more
than a multicolored blanket, Lance asked, "How is
she?"

"The crying helped. She needed to do that. I
think seeing his . . . his body confirmed his death
in her mind." She licked her lips and asked, "Was
he . . . ?"

"No. It was a merciful murder," he said bitterly.
"The coroner's report named asphyxiation as cause
of death. They probably smothered him in his sleep
by placing a pillow over his face."

She covered her mouth with one hand and paled
considerably but didn't say anything. She stared
straight ahead. "I'm grateful to him for having written that letter," she said musingly. "Whatever its
contents, it seemed to reassure her of his love."

"Yes. I'm glad the burglars saw fit to leave that
behind."

"Do they have any suspects?"

"No. It will go down as one of those unsolvable

murders. Burglary was the motive. He—or they—were in and out in minutes. Obviously professional. Of course, we're lucky that they missed the money under the bed.''

"Yes, aren't we though," she sneered. An uncontrollable urge to hurt him seized her. She wanted to punish him for treating her the way he had the night before. She wanted him to suffer under verbal attacks the way he had made her suffer.

"You should be very proud of yourself, Mr. Barrett. You can go home the hero now. What do you say when you've succeeded in ruining someone's life? 'Well, boys, we can close the cover on this one.' Or maybe, 'Wrap this one up'?''

It wasn't fair. She knew it wasn't. He hadn't been responsible for Ken's crime. But she was hurt. She would never see her brother. All her dreams of establishing family ties, sharing, finding affection, had been cruelly dashed. She wanted to lash out at something, someone, for the pain she was feeling. Lance was there. It wasn't fair, but she felt a perverse sense of satisfaction at seeing the lines around his mouth tighten. His eyebrows lowered over glowering eyes.

To escape that hard stare, she leaned her head back on the seat cushion and shut her eyes. A few minutes later, she felt rather than heard him stop a flight attendant as she made her way up the aisle.

Lance nudged her elbow and ordered, "Here, drink this.''

He was holding a glass of liquor. "What is it?''

"Brandy. You need it."

She shook her head no. "I don't drink anything that strong."

He looked at her scornfully, then said, "Well I do." He gulped the first glass of the amber liquid and tears came to his eyes. He made a terrible face and sucked in his breath when the fiery liquor hit his stomach, but then he lay his head back and closed his eyes. "You really should try it. It does wonders for the nerves." He sipped at the other glass slowly.

For long moments neither of them spoke. When he did, his voice was softer. "I'm sorry about Lyman, Erin. I wouldn't have had it end this way."

She turned her head to face him. His eyes met hers across the inches of dusty upholstery that separated them. "I know," she whispered. "What I said before was foolish and unfair. Forgive me?"

For an answer, he reached out and took her hand. He passed his brandy glass to a flight attendant, then moved into the middle seat next to the one by the window in which Erin sat. He raised the armrest separating them. Very few lights remained on inside the aircraft. The few passengers on board were either sleeping or using the dim overhead lights above their seats. The flight attendants, after having seen to everyone's comfort, had retired to their assigned stations.

With her hand lying in the palm of his, he examined it with the fingers of his other hand. He traced the long, oval nails, the knuckles, and the fine delicate veins on the backs of her hand. His knee was pressing companionably against hers. Somehow her shoulder had come under the protection of his.

"Tell me about your husband, Erin." The request was made quietly, almost inconsequentially.

She didn't pretend ignorance. Giving in to an irresistible urge, she lay her head on his shoulder. "Joseph was the kindest man I'd ever met. He was immensely successful in business. Part of his success stemmed from the fact that his employees adored him. He gave even the lowliest mail clerk a share in the profits. Some may accuse him of being a shrewd manager, but I think that he really wanted to distribute his wealth."

Lance raised his arm and put it around her shoulders, pulling her closer. Her head rested on his chest. "When he first started showing an interest in me, I thought it was because he valued my judgments, my knowledge of his business. And he did. But it was only after we had had several dinner dates that I realized he was seeing me because he liked me. In retrospect, I think I recaptured his youth. He had been widowed for many years. His children were grown and led their own busy lives. For a long time, his business had been his only interest in life. He was lonely.

"Anyway, he asked me to marry him. I was stunned and a little frightened. He had always been so scrupulously mannerly that his proposal took me completely off guard. I consented, not because I loved him, at least not romantically, but because I thought he would be hurt if I refused.''

Her hand had found its way to Lance's thigh, and she was running her finger up and down the crease in his trouser leg. ''I married him, much to everyone's dismay. I think my name was bandied about as being an opportunist, a gold digger. I didn't like people thinking badly of me, but I knew my motives were above reproach. I couldn't let other uninformed opinions affect me or Joseph. I was young, lonely, and just a little flattered that such an important man could love me. That's all there was to it. He died later that same year.''

Lance captured her hand with his and pressed it against the muscle of his leg. ''Not quite all, Erin.''

His tone was so intimate that she blushed. She raised her eyes briefly. He was leaning down over her so closely that their faces nearly came into contact. His blue eyes speared through her own. She returned her head to his chest.

''The marriage was never consummated. Joseph—he tried, but—he was already sick,'' she stammered. Her face was flaming scarlet. ''When he went to a doctor to check on—uh—the other, they discovered the malignancy. It was inoperable.''

Returning her thoughts to those sad days after Joseph's death, Erin was made aware of the change she had undergone since meeting Lance. After Joseph's embarrassing attempts to make her his wife in the physical sense, she had become afraid of sex. He had been so completely devastated when he couldn't perform as a husband that Erin had felt his pain and embarrassment just as keenly as he had. She never wanted anything to do with sex again. It couldn't be worth the price of sacrificing someone's self-esteem.

She hadn't become involved with a man again. It wasn't for lack of invitation. Many men in New York had pursued her before and after her marriage to Joseph, but she had managed to bridle their passions until they became frustrated enough to seek other partners. In Houston, much the same thing had happened until she met Bart and they had finally reached an understanding about her not sleeping with him.

It wasn't the act itself that frightened her. The O'Sheas had been a loving couple with a healthy, active sex life. Even as a child, Erin had discerned that her parents shared something special.

Her problem was a fear of being disillusioned again if things went wrong.

Why then had she accepted Lance Barrett so readily? Since that first embrace when she still thought him to be Ken, she had felt a desire kindling and igniting until it raged inside her like a forest fire. Even when she was flinging aspersions in his face, she had had to fight that forceful sexual awareness of him.

And he had known it. Her body hadn't been able to keep its longing a secret and his had instinctively responded. Unconsciously she had exuded a magnetic current that he hadn't ignored or resisted.

She was playing a dangerous game. Part of her reason for refusing to be Bart's mistress had been her compulsive desire for a family. Somehow, she had known that Bart wasn't what she wanted in the way of a husband and father to her children. Becoming too involved with him might put a stumbling block in the way of her achieving what she wanted most out of her life.

If Bart was a stumbling block, Lance was a mountain. A few days from now they would go their separate ways and never see each other again. Why was she gambling her future? A brief affair with Lance led nowhere. It was stupid. It was hopeless. It was immoral.

Yet now, when she could feel his breath against her cheek and the pressure of his arm against the soft cushion of her breast, she also knew that it was ordained and out of her control.

She lifted her head and looked at him. He drowned in the depths of her dark eyes that were wide and liquid with the train of her thoughts. His lips compressed into a stern line when he said, "I'm sorry for what happened last night in the park."

"You were angry," she replied simply. "I knew that."

"That's no excuse for what I almost did. God! Rape." He sighed in self-disgust. "I've never been violent with a woman, Erin. Believe me. Did I hurt you?" The guilty look on his face melted her heart.

"A little," she said with a smile.

"I wish it had never happened. If I could undo it, I would."

"Why don't you apologize?" she suggested seductively.

He smiled down at her tenderly and placed his index finger on her lips. He moved it from one corner of her mouth to the other with a slow, provocative stroke. "Erin, I apologize for my beastly behavior."

"Your apology is accepted," she whispered. His finger lowered her bottom lip and raked against her teeth.

Furtively, he glanced around him. "I wish we weren't in so public a place," he grumbled.

"Why? What would you do if we weren't?"

"E . . . Erin." He said her name through gritted teeth as she caught his finger in her mouth and sucked on it gently. "If your hand comes any farther up my thigh, you'll know beyond a shadow of a doubt what I would do."

"What would you do," she challenged breathlessly.

He picked up the thrown gauntlet. "I'd probably kiss you like this."

He kept one arm firmly around her and, with the other hand, cradled her face as he lowered his lips to hers. At first he teased her, biting gently on her lips, painting them with his tongue. He pulled back slightly to review the results of his torment. Her eyes were partially veiled with her black-fringed lids and her breath was escaping through parted lips, shiny and wet with the lubricant of his own mouth.

"Erin," he breathed as his lips closed over hers. Now was not the time to solve their problems. What if she did have a fiancé who was a millionaire? She wasn't wearing his damn diamond ring now. He knew almost to the minute when she had taken off that symbol of another man's claim.

What if he would never see her again? What if her income quadrupled his? What the hell did any of that matter now?

She was here. It was dark and cozy and they needed each other. Her body was supple and gave in to the demands of his. Her dear hand lay only inches from that part of him that knew her intimately and strained to know her again. Her lips were opened and receptive to his searching tongue. He had a hard time restraining a moan that formed in his chest and pushed up to clog his throat.

"You taste like brandy." The kiss was over, but their lips were still touching. "From now on, I'll love brandy."

"Drink some more," he said. This time it was her tongue that explored his mouth, finding all the hollows and filling them. When she pulled away, she teased the cleft in his chin with that relentless tongue which left him feeling weak and conversely powerful.

Her index finger replaced her tongue in that intriguing crevice as she asked huskily, "And if you got away with kissing me like that, then what would you do?"

He was all too eager now to participate in this duel of the senses. He put on his stern government agent face and said, "I'm not convinced that you're not some hardened criminal hiding behind a sexy disguise. Especially now that you've tried to seduce me, my suspicions are aroused."

"That's not all that's aroused," she said in a barely audible singsong voice.

Did she actually brush her hand over him or was that only his overactive imagination? Hell, the way he felt now, anything was possible. He swallowed hard and grated, "You're getting me off the subject."

"I'm sorry, sir," she said contritely. "Please continue."

"As I was saying," he cleared his throat authoritatively, "I'd probably feel the need to search you again."

His mouth took on an insolent slant that she remembered all too well. When she had first seen it, the arrogant expression had frightened her. Now she found that it caused her heart to pound with excitement.

"You surely wouldn't want to be derelict in your duty," she said solemnly.

"No. I couldn't let that happen." He brought his face down to hers again, but he didn't kiss her. Instead he looked deeply into her eyes as he slipped his hand under her blazer. It lay warm and heavy against her chest, similar to the warm heaviness that centered in the lower part of her body and throbbed between her thighs. With agonizing slowness, he moved his hand downward.

Erin was held spellbound by the flashing sensations that radiated from his fingers through her blouse to her skin. His eyes impaled her. They held her in a tender, but avaricious, gaze. He couldn't get enough of her.

His palm settled over her breast and molded it to his hand. Sensuously he began massaging her in a circular rhythm until he felt her become taut and firm in the center of his hand. The lips he was watching so hungrily parted and formed his name.

"You have two very feminine habits, Erin O'Shea," he said with infinite softness. "One of them is this." He brushed his thumb over the responsive crest. "The other is saying my name without really saying it. I find them both endearing."

He left her only long enough to set free two of her buttons. Then it was the flesh of his hand sliding over the lush curves. As gently as if he were undressing an infant, he pushed aside the wispy lace barrier of her bra and surrounded her with his hand.

She leaned forward, making herself fuller, more accessible to him. But never did their eyes waver. Hers became shuttered momentarily when his thumb began its own distinct finessing.

He leaned over her and placed his lips against her ear. After kissing it and the velvet, scented skin around it, he whispered, "Erin, God help me, but I want you." His words were urgent, but if anything, his questing hand became more soothing.

Rolling her nipple between sensitive fingers, he asked, "Did I tell you what a pretty color you are? I can remember just what this feels like in my mouth, against my tongue, what you taste like. Right now, I want—"

The seat belt sign lit up and they heard the soft chimes that called attention to it. Lance's breath was expulsed near her ear with a muffled curse. He eased away from her and, protecting her with his body, rebuttoned her blouse before returning to sit straight in his own seat.

She reached out tentatively to touch his arm, but he hissed, "Don't touch me." When he saw her hurt expression, he smiled. "Hasn't it occurred to you that it may take a minute or two for me to become decent again?" He looked at her with a lopsided grin until she caught his meaning. When she did, she jerked her hand back and faced the front of the airplane, not daring to move. He chuckled deeply.

Just when the wheels of the aircraft skidded to the runway, she looked at him shyly. "Lance, do you . . . do you think I'm terrible for acting so shamelessly in light of what happened today? Am I a disgraceful person?"

His smile was gentle and sincere. "It's been my experience over the years to watch the reactions of people in all sorts of chaotic situations. I've discovered that an emotional release from tension or grief can take myriad forms. Some people weep, or scream, or get angry. Others laugh uncontrollably. Some turn to love.'' He paused significantly. ''One emotion is as honest as the next, Erin.''

''Thank you,'' she murmured.

CHAPTER

Ten

"Hello, Aunt Reba. This is Erin. Is Mother there?"

"Erin! We were just talking about you. Are you back in Houston?"

"No. I'm calling from San Francisco."

"Well, I won't keep you. Your mother is dying to talk to you. Good-bye, dear."

The funeral would take place in an hour, but Erin needed to talk to her mother so desperately that she took the time to place the long distance call.

Yesterday had been the grimmest day Erin had ever spent in her life. Melanie had decided not to delay Ken's funeral. It was planned for four o'clock in the afternoon, barely allowing time for all the preparations to be made. The decision was a wise one, Erin thought. The sooner Melanie could restore her life to some semblance of normalcy, the better.

"Hello, Erin." Merle O'Shea's cheerful voice was like a balm on Erin's wounded spirit.

"Mother, it's so good to hear your voice. How are you?"

"I'm fine. But more to the point, how are you? You sound unhappy."

That was all the encouragement Erin needed. The whole story came gushing out amid a torrent of tears. She began with her arrival on Ken Lyman's doorstep and ended with the funeral taking place that afternoon. She sobbed brokenly into the telephone.

"Oh, my darling girl, I'm so sorry for you. I can't even imagine how horrible this has all been. Especially when you were looking so forward to finding and meeting your brother." Erin heard her mother's voice crack. As always, when Erin was hurt, so was her adoptive mother. Erin hadn't grown in her womb, but she had certainly grown in her heart.

"Is there something I can do? Would you like for me to come to San Francisco?"

That would be a supreme sacrifice. Merle O'Shea was terrified of flying. "No, Mother. It's helped so much just to talk to you. Really, I'll be fine. I have to be for Melanie's sake."

"She sounds like such a sweet girl."

"She is. We really feel like sisters."

Her mother stumbled over her next question. "Erin, did—I mean did you find any information about your—real mother?"

Erin smiled into the receiver. Her mother couldn't help a little spark of maternal jealousy. "No, Mother, I didn't."

"I'll never forgive myself for destroying those records they gave me at the orphanage before I even read them. When Gerald and I got you, I was so thrilled and so selfishly possessive of you—"

"Mother, please. We've been through this a thousand times. At the time, you felt that you were doing the right thing for me. Besides, I'm not sure I want to know anything more now. I don't think I could stand another disappointment."

Each of them was lost in thought for a moment before Merle asked, "This Mr. Barrett, is he nice? I hope he's not some insensitive tough guy."

Erin had deliberately refrained from any mention of her personal involvement with Lance Barrett. Was he nice? "Yes, he's nice, I suppose, though he's handled everything very professionally. I wouldn't call him insensitive."

Her mother seemed satisfied with her answer. "Good. You have that to be thankful for."

"Yes."

"When are you coming home, Erin? I'll feel so much better when you're back in Houston. You won't seem so far away."

Erin sighed. She hadn't made any plans to go home, though she knew now that she must. "I don't know, Mother," she answered honestly. "I want to make sure that Melanie is going to be all right. Within a few days for sure. I'll let you know."

"Please do." Merle paused for a long moment; then she said, "Erin, I know how much this meant to you. If I could spare you this heartache, I would. You know that, don't you?"

"Yes, Mother."

"Sometimes things happen in our lives for which there isn't an explanation. I hope this hasn't lessened your faith that God takes care of you."

"No. I need that faith now more than ever."

"You'll be in my prayers. I love you, Erin."

"I love you, too. Good-bye, Mother."

"Good-bye."

Erin replaced the receiver, hating to break that communicating thread with the loving woman who had given her life, if not birth.

Listlessly, she returned to the guest bedroom to finish dressing for the funeral. In Houston, she had packed a simple Halston dress of black wool jersey to wear to dinner should the occasion arise. Now she was wearing it to a funeral. Black textured hose and black suede pumps completed her outfit. Her only adornments were a pair of pearl studs in her ears and a strand of pearls around her neck.

Erin looked good in black and wore it often. It complemented her dark hair and eyes and her fair complexion. But Melanie wasn't so fortunate. The black dress she had borrowed from Charlotte Winslow wrapped around her like a shroud. Her fair hair was still peeled away from her face in a severe style. The black dress made her wan complexion look even more sallow. Her eyes, which Erin had seen sparkle with childlike excitement, were lackluster and vacant.

It was a strange cortege that proceeded from the house to the chapel in the cemetery. Erin and Melanie rode in the somber limousine provided by the funeral director. They were accompanied by Melanie's parents, who appeared annoyed by the whole affair. Disparagingly, Erin wondered if the funeral had conflicted with a bridge tournament or a golf game and inconvenienced Melanie's parents.

Lance, Mike, and Clark followed at a sedate pace in their unmarked government car.

Melanie seemed to have cried herself dry last night before boarding the airplane. After landing, when Erin and Lance had roused her, she had remained composed, if somewhat aloof. She withstood the funeral service stoically.

A grief she hadn't experienced since the death of Gerald O'Shea washed over Erin as she looked at the unpretentious coffin covered with the spray of copper chrysanthemums that contained her brother's body.

She had come so close to knowing and loving him. So close, and yet she would never see him alive. Never hear his voice. Never enjoy the nuances of his personality. Had she entered his life a few days earlier, could her appearance have altered the course he had taken? Would her existence have made a difference in his life?

During the funeral service, she performed much like Melanie. She was vague and disoriented, mired down in a miasma of despair.

It was almost dark by the time they returned to

the Lyman residence. Erin went upstairs with Melanie and left her at the door of her room. Before she did anything else, Erin wanted to take off the black dress. She doubted she would ever wear it again.

She put on the old jeans she had worn her first night in the house and a comfortable sweater. She brushed her hair and repaired her face, which had been marred by streaking makeup. Feeling somewhat better, she decided that, even though she wasn't hungry, she should eat some of the food that friends and neighbors had brought to the house. She was still having some residual weakness from her illness and hadn't eaten properly in the last three days.

At the bottom of the stairs she stood awestruck as she saw Melanie coming down the steps carrying two suitcases.

"Melanie, what—"

"Erin, this is probably the rudest thing I've ever done in my life, but I've got to leave you here."

Erin was stunned by her calm announcement. "Bu—but where are you going? Why?"

"Did you hear my parents?"

It would have been hard not to, Erin wanted to say. The Winslows had accompanied their daughter home from the funeral and immediately upon entering the house had started railing at her to come home with them. They had caused quite a scene, embarrassing the young widow.

"I told them that I wanted to spend the night in

my own house, especially since you would still be here. But I promised that tomorrow I would move back home.'' Melanie's lips formed a resolute straight line. ''That's a promise I have no intention of keeping. They've ruined my life, not to mention Ken's. I'm not giving them the opportunity to go on controlling me.''

Erin glanced around in desperation and saw Lance standing behind her. He was listening to Melanie's declaration. ''But where will you go tonight?'' Erin asked, grasping at straws.

''I don't know,'' Melanie shrugged with disinterest. ''I really don't care. Just away from here. From them.'' She sighed sadly. ''I really don't want to sell the house just now, but I can't stay here and be subjected to their constant badgering. Do you understand?''

It was a plea for assurance. In spite of her misgivings about the advisability of Melanie's plans, Erin said, ''Of course I understand.''

''Thank you, Erin. I knew you would. I'm leaving a letter for my parents on the entrance hall table. Please give it to them when they come for me tomorrow.''

''Is there anything else?''

''No. I'll contact you soon. I wrote down your address and telephone number in Houston. I hate to run out on a guest like this, but it's something I have to do.''

Erin smiled. ''I'm not a guest. I'm family.''

"Is there anything you need, Mrs. Lyman? Do you have any money?" Lance asked quietly from behind Erin. He endorsed Melanie's leaving.

"Yes. I have a personal account. I hate to give you any more responsibility, Mr. Barrett, but when you have cleared out all your equipment, would you leave the key to the house with the next door neighbor? She's expecting it. She agreed to look after things for me until I come back."

"It's done," he stated firmly.

Impulsively, Melanie walked toward him. The next instant she was enclosed in his arms. "Thank you for being so nice about everything," Erin heard her mumble into his shirt front. "I know you did everything you possibly could to find Ken and bring him back. You would have dealt with him justly."

Lance squeezed his eyes shut tightly. "I wouldn't have had it happen like this for anything in the world, Mrs. Lyman." Melanie withdrew to the door, then turned to face them.

"In a way I'm glad that Ken didn't have to go to prison or suffer any more indignities. He had been unhappy for a long time. In his letter to me," she touched her breast where Erin guessed the unmailed missive was secreted, "he says he was looking for acceptance. I think he took the money to get the world's attention as though saying, 'I'm alive. Here I am, Kenneth Lyman.' I'm no philosopher or psychologist, but I see his motives so clearly now. And I know he loved me, despite everything."

Out of the mouths of babes, Erin thought, and

tears rolled unchecked down her cheeks as she clasped this dear sister-in-law to her one more time. She and Lance stood by the front door as Melanie backed her car out of the garage and, with a poignant wave, drove off into the night.

"Do you think she'll be all right, Lance?" Erin asked anxiously.

"Far better than she's been," he murmured, and Erin found comfort in his simple words. "Here," he said, looking at her with an amused grin. "Let me wipe your face." He extracted a white handkerchief from his hip pocket and blotted her tears. "How long has it been since you had a decent meal?"

"I can't remember," she laughed.

"That's what I thought," he said grimly. "You're getting skinny." As if to show her, he placed his hands on her ribs and steered her in the direction of the kitchen. "There's enough food in here for an army, and we'll have to throw it away in the morning. So let's dig in."

While she was filling her plate in the kitchen, he went into the living room and picked up the red telephone. "Mike, tell the boys to take a break and come eat some of this food."

He was tieless and his sleeves were rolled up to his elbows when he walked back into the kitchen. "You haven't got enough," he said, inspecting her plate like a schoolmaster. Over her protests, he added another piece of cold fried chicken and a scoop of potato salad.

"I'll get fat," she wailed as he continued to pile food onto her plate.

He grinned that open, friendly, teasing smile that was so rare, but so captivating. "Not a chance. Besides, I know a *couple* of places that could stand some plumping out." His eyes dropped meaningfully to her breasts.

"I—" she opened her mouth to rebuke his audacity, but the back door swung open and his men trooped in. She recognized only Mike and Clark, but there were three others. She was certain they had seen her and knew that they had overheard her conversation with Bart. She blushed as Lance introduced them.

They were all uptight, overly polite, and far too quiet. Erin finally figured out that their obsequious manner was in deference to her. There had been a funeral today and each of them was all too aware of the circumstances. For her own sake as well as theirs, she set about to alleviate the gloom.

She began asking them polite questions and before long they were responding to her openly without first darting a permission-seeking look at Lance. Then they began to contribute to the dialogue, and by the time they left, there had even been some spontaneous laughter.

Erin gathered up the used paper plates and disposable utensils and stuffed them in a plastic trash bag. Lance insisted on helping her wash out the containers of food. After his crew was finished, not too much had been wasted.

"I guess I'll have to take these dishes over to the neighbor in the morning. She can return them to their owners."

"I guess so," Erin said as she wiped off the counter top with a damp sponge. She didn't want to ask, but had to. "When will you be leaving?"

Lance didn't answer for a while. He was inordinately busy twisting a tie around the top of the garbage bag and placing it near the back door to be taken out in the morning. "We're shaking down all our stuff tonight. I have a few loose ends to tie up. If not tomorrow, probably the next day. You?"

Erin looked away. She took off the apron she had put around her waist and hung it on a peg in the pantry. "I don't know. I was planning to stay a few days with Melanie, but now . . ." Her voice trailed off to nothing.

When she turned around, he was standing close to her. He placed his hands on her shoulders and gently massaged the tense cords of her neck. "You're exhausted," he whispered solicitously. "I've got to gather up some papers in the living room. I'll lock up when I leave. You go on upstairs."

It was a dismissal. She hadn't really known what to expect from him, but she thought it would have been more than a good night one would have given a kid sister.

Just as she reached the door going into the hallway, he said, "Erin?" Her heart thudded with joy, and she whirled around to face him. He wasn't even looking at her. Instead he was staring out the window. "Yes?" *Lance, turn around!* her heart screamed.

"If you need anything during the night, pick up the red telephone. We won't disconnect it until the morning."

That was it? That was all he had to say?

"Okay," she responded despondently and trudged up the stairs.

She got ready for bed mechanically, taking no interest in what she was doing. When she climbed between the sheets, the bed, the room, the house felt as cold and empty as her heart.

It all makes sense, Erin, she chided herself. After all, what had she expected? He was on a job. Tomorrow that job would be completed. He would go back to Washington and await his next assignment. Erin O'Shea would probably be mentioned in the dossier he would turn in, and sometimes in the future he might fondly recall her, but he would soon forget their shared passion. His memory of her face would wane.

He had found her mildly amusing during a difficult case. She provided a diversion from the pressures that went with his job.

But how could he dismiss her so summarily? Didn't he even remember what had happened in this room? This bed? The very walls of the small room seemed to echo the garbled, frantic words he had rasped in her ear. To her they had sounded like a love song.

Foolish! Stupid! she berated herself.

Yet she could still hear him. "Oh, sweet . . . You're ready . . . Perfect, perfect . . . You feel . . . Erin, I'll wait . . . Erin . . . Erin . . . Erin . . ."

It was very late when she woke up, probably after midnight. The house was still and quiet, but she couldn't go back to sleep. After straightening the covers, using the bathroom, and tossing her head on the pillow for a few restless minutes, she decided that she needed a drink of cold water.

Getting out of bed once again, she slipped on a robe, but didn't bother with slippers. Without turning on any lights, she crept down the stairs. At the bottom, she gasped.

The house was on fire!

For a panic-stricken moment, her hand clasped the top of her robe at her throat. Her heart was racing. But as the seconds ticked by, she realized that she was wrong. She didn't smell any smoke and the fire was localized in the paneled study.

On trembling knees, she walked down the dark hallway and looked in the room. There were no lights on, but a fire was burning brightly in the grate of the fireplace, unused until now.

Puzzled, she stepped across the threshold and then came to an abrupt halt. Lance was sprawled in the chair he had slept in once before. An empty glass was held in his dangling hand. A bottle of brandy was on the table at his elbow.

Cautiously she moved farther into the room. He

was sleeping soundly. She smiled tenderly to see his eyeglasses resting on the top of his head. His tousled hair shone golden in the firelight.

On silent feet she tiptoed closer, studying his face in repose. Her heart swelled with love. Love? *Yes!* She loved him. And it was gloriously right and painfully wrong. For a million reasons, it was wrong, but at that moment, her reasonable mind's objections were overshadowed, consumed, obliterated by the love that suffused her.

Hoping not to awaken him, she reached out her hand and picked the glasses off his head. He didn't stir. She set them on the table. His hair was springy and alive as the firelight danced on it. The temptation to touch it was too potent to resist.

The burnished strands felt like spun silk between her fingers as she brushed away a contrary lock that lay on his forehead. His eyes opened.

For what seemed an eternity they were held in suspended animation. Not daring to breathe and break this mesmerizing spell, they were content to absorb each other with unquenchable eyes.

He didn't move any part of his body except his hand. He raised it and grasped Erin's hand that was still poised above his head. His fingers closed firm and warm around hers. He brought her hand to his cheek and pressed it against that lean plane. Moving his jaw only slightly, he nuzzled her palm with his mouth until she felt his tongue in its center. Then he was kissing it with a fervor that intimated other love play.

Slowly, as if they were players acting out a dream, he drew her down onto his lap. The glass he was holding in his hand dropped to the rug with a soft thud. Her bottom fit snugly in his lap, her legs draped over his right thigh. Pushing aside the collar of her robe, he buried his face in the hollow of her neck.

"Erin, if you're a dream, I hope I never wake up." His voice was urgent and hot with desire.

She threw her head back and allowed his seeking lips more access to her throat and chest. "Lance, I'm no dream. I'm all too human. Lance—" His lips voraciously devoured hers. She was crushed against his chest as he encircled her with his arms. The hard drumming of his heart pounded in her ear. Their mouths melted together, fired by a torch that seared their souls.

"You taste like brandy again," she said, nibbling at his lips. "Are you getting hooked on that stuff?"

"I'm hooked on this," he mumbled while doing wonderful things to her ear with his tongue. "And this," he said, raining soft kisses on the features of her face. "And this." Now he was moving his chin down her chest. "And this," he groaned against her breasts. One of his hands cupped her gently. Then he smoothed that hand over her stomach and abdomen and placed his palm over the mound where her lap curved into her thighs. "And this." He pressed his hand against her intimately, molding his hand to the intricacies of her body with unerring accuracy.

Her limbs quivered and a fountain bubbled within her, making her moist and pliant with unconstrained longing. Her body sought more of his, drawing him closer by wrapping her arms around his neck.

He stayed her by gripping both her shoulders and looking deeply into her eyes. "Erin, I want you tonight more than I've ever wanted a woman in my life. But I could never live with myself if I took advantage of you—anyone—when you are as vulnerable as you are right now. Today your emotions have been running high, close to the surface. Are you sure this is what you want?"

For an answer her hands took his and eased them gently off her shoulders. Then she shrugged out of her robe. He drew his breath in sharply when he saw her nightgown. It was the one he had commented on while rifling through her suitcase that first day in this room. The pale blue silk highlighted the opalescence of her skin. The ecru lace that comprised the bodice fit tight across her breasts and left nothing to the imagination.

"Erin—" he choked.

Made courageous by his obvious appreciation, she pulled down the satin strap first off one shoulder, then the other. In a matter of heartbeats, the garment formed a frothy pool of lace around her waist.

He revered her with worshipful eyes. The firelight bathed her body with a golden glow and haloed her hair with shimmering light. She was the most beautiful creature he had ever seen. And the most ethereal. He asked himself again if she was real.

To satisfy his mind that she was, his index finger reached out to brush the pink crest of her breast. He watched in fascination as it responded. Lowering his head he touched the distended nipple with the tip of his tongue. He heard her sighing his name over the cacophonous cadence of his own heart. As he knew it wouldn't be, one taste of her wasn't enough. His mouth covered the taut peak and drew from her breast a flavor more intoxicating than the brandy.

He stood up, lifting her with him, and as he did, her nightgown floated to the floor. Taking a few steps backward, he eased her down on the rug directly in front of the fireplace.

It surprised him, as it had before, when she watched so unabashedly while he undressed. For the first time in his adult life, he was self-conscious of his body. Her eager hands, clasping him to her when he lay beside her, dispelled any fears that she might not find him appealing.

He kissed her deeply, pressing her malleable body along the hard length of his. The logs popped in the fireplace. Their music was sweet accompaniment to the love words being exchanged.

Erin had never experienced this sense of helpless surrender, yet she reveled in it. Lance conquered her body, mind, and soul, but there was no protestation from her. His hands and mouth were weapons he wielded with precision, but the conquest was executed with excruciating tenderness.

He loved her in ways before unimagined. Kneeling at the gate of her womanhood, he stroked her, kissed her, coaxed her to the edge of fulfillment, but then led her back before she slipped over the brink, only to heighten her passion again and again.

Her hands wandered over his large frame with wondrous curiosity. She watched the hard muscles under her fingertips twitch with unleashed desire as she leisurely explored them. His nipples became aroused under her delicate manipulation. Shyness overcame her as her hand lowered beyond the point of his navel that nestled in silky, golden hair.

His whole body went rigid with anticipation. He waited. Then his pent-up breath was released in a long shuddering sigh when she timidly touched him.

"Yes, Erin. Touch me. Don't ever be afraid of me. Never. Touch me. Touch me . . ."

His uneven words imbued her with confidence and a need to return the bliss he had given her. She grew bolder and closed her hands around him in a way she hoped was pleasing. The pulsating force she felt beneath her fingers and his gasping endearments were proof enough that her temerity was rewarded.

Covering her hands with his own, he held her against him and whispered thickly, "You weave a magic I've never known before, Erin. You are . . . you . . ."

He couldn't finish. Their fusion was sweet, swift, and absolute. A moment later while they lay still, savoring the depth of their embrace, he raised his head and looked deeply into her slumberous eyes.

"You are the magic."

"Hey, sleepyhead."

Erin stirred against the warm body next to hers and mumbled a protest. She slid her thigh over the hairy leg beside her.

"We'd better get up," Lance said close to her ear. His action belied his words as he nibbled her earlobe lazily.

"No," Erin muttered into her pillow as she snuggled closer to him, brushing his chest with her breasts.

"Have you forgotten that I'm a very important man around here?" His hand couldn't resist an inquisitive research of that soft cushion of flesh that came to life under his playful fingers. "My men are depending on me for leadership. I can't lie in bed with an insatiable broad all day."

She slapped him on his firm buttock. "Who's insatiable?" she asked, raising her head slightly to nuzzle his neck. Her knee inched higher up his thigh and she got the expected response. He rolled her over and kissed her expansively, drinking her mouth like a man dying of thirst. Just when she was becoming liquid and pliable in his arms, he released her lips and rested his forehead against hers.

"You'd tempt a saint, Erin O'Shea, but dammit, I do have to get up. It's almost eight o'clock." He swung his legs over the side of the bed. They had moved to the guest bedroom sometime during the night. Lance pulled on a pair of daringly sexy underwear.

Erin, her skin naked and glowing with the aftermath of a night of love, scooted over to the edge of the bed and wrapped her arms around his waist, resting her cheek against his flat abdomen.

"Lance," she whined, "do you have to get up so early?" Errantly, her hands smoothed over the taut muscles of his hips and down the backs of his legs. The sensitive skin inside his thighs was tormented by trailing fingertips. Her breasts pressed against him with a shocking intimacy.

"Erin—" he broke off with a startled intake of breath when he felt the tip of her tongue on his bare skin. Trying to regain some measure of his slipping control, he threatened in a severe voice, "Erin, you're asking for it."

She looked up at him triumphantly and nodded. "Um-hum." Gradually she lowered the fragile cloth that was straining its limits.

He tried to suppress the smile that broke across his chiseled lips. "You know what my motto is?"

She shook her head, brushing him with her hair. "No. What?"

"Always give the people what they want." The mattress sank under his weight as he fell across it and hungrily gathered her into his arms.

He left her drowsing in bed while he showered, shaved, and dressed. He leaned over and pecked her on the cheek. "I'll go brew some coffee."

Her eyes were filled with love as she nodded and said, "I'll be down shortly."

When he pulled the door closed behind him, Erin stretched like a contented feline and then burrowed her head into the pillow Lance had used, breathing deeply of his scent that still clung to the linens.

Was love always like this? Did everyone else in the whole world know about this exquisite thrill that rocketed through her veins and electrified each nerve of her body? Could her heart stand to swell any larger with love for this man?

Last night had gone beyond even her wildest fantasies of what loving a man could mean. Their physical intimacies had not been tainted by inhibition or shame. The tempo was varied, one time being fierce and ravenous, the next leisurely and tender, postponing the crescendo until it, of its own accord, crashed around them.

And in between those bouts of ecstasy, they

shared their innermost fears, dreams, and philosophies. Childhoods were reminisced, and vignettes from adolescent years were laughed over. Trivia was made vastly important. Each was voracious for knowledge of the other.

In everything he did, Erin felt Lance's love. Each look, each touch transmitted the emotion, though it hadn't been spoken in so mundane a form as language.

As she hopped from the bed, her eagerness to see him again renewing her recently expended energy, she knew his declaration of love was only a matter of time. He wouldn't let her sift out of his life now. Somehow they would manage two diverse lifestyles, two separate careers. They would work it out. They had to.

Lance. Lance Barrett. Lawrence Barrett. She loved the name and shouted it to the walls of the tile shower over the whishing sound of water.

She put on a pair of black wool slacks, but feeling utterly feminine and wanting to look it, topped them with a pink georgette blouse. Lace inserts flanked the collar and allowed a tantalizing glimpse of her creamy skin underneath. She dabbed a provocative fragrance behind her ears and down her throat, then impulsively scented the cleavage between her breasts. They were still tingling with remembered caresses.

Downstairs she spoke to Mike, who was helping a telephone company representative disconnect the red telephone. He looked at her and smiled, saying a cheerful good morning. Did he know where Lance had spent the night? Did she care if he knew? No! The aroma of fresh perked coffee led her toward the kitchen. Lance was standing at the counter buttering slices of toast.

She went up behind him and put her arms around his waist. "Good morning, Mr. Barrett," she chimed primly. Her hand slipped under his belt.

"Good morning, Miss O'Shea. I trust you had a restful night." He settled his bottom against her middle.

She giggled. "Not exactly restful, but most pleasant, thank you." She added on a low, seductive note, "For everything." Her hand separated the front of his shirt under his trousers and touched his warm vibrance with fingers not lacking in boldness.

The knife he was using clattered to the counter top. "Miss O'Shea, perhaps I should warn . . . ahhh, Erin . . . warn you it's against the law to acc—accost an agent of the federal government." The unsteadiness of his voice matched his labored breathing.

"Is it?" she taunted.

"Yes." He drew a sharp breath. "Oh hell," he said through clenched teeth. "And you'd better stop what you're doing or—"

"Or what?" she challenged.

He spun around to face her. Placing a strong arm behind her back he drew her against him until she could feel the results of her teasing. His eyes gleamed with desire as he growled, "Or you know what.'' Then he kissed her fully, but quickly, on the mouth and pushed her away from him. He raked her with his eyes appraisingly.

''How can you look so angelic when I know that under that pure, innocent exterior beats the heart of a consummate wanton?''

She placed her fists on her hips, a gesture that pulled the fabric of her blouse tight across her breasts in a revealing, evocative display. ''What a dastardly thing to say,'' she said haughtily. ''I'll have you know—''

''What?''

''I'll have you know,'' she smiled mischievously, ''that you are absolutely right.'' She raised her face toward his descending lips, but the doorbell peeled loudly.

''You have been saved by the bell, Miss O'Shea, from a fate worse than death.''

''Damn.''

''Go see who it is. Mike is busy and I need to get this toast finished. For some reason I have quite an appetite this morning.''

''You have quite an appetite for a lot of things.'' She winked lasciviously.

He swatted her playfully on the bottom as he shooed her out of the kitchen.

She was still smiling abstractedly when she pulled open the front door. ''*Bart!*'' she shrieked when she saw her fiancé standing across the threshold.

''Hi, sugar,'' he said shyly. ''I didn't mean to startle you. I didn't expect you to answer the door.''

Erin had gone drastically pale and her heart had lurched up to her throat. She hadn't even thought of Bart in hours. Days? Certainly not since last night. Seeing him standing here now was an unpleasant shock.

"Baby, I know what hell you've been through, but I'm tired. Can I come in?"

She was still too stunned to think rationally, but she answered, "Oh—of course. I'm sorry. It—I'm just surprised to see you, that's all."

He came in the hallway and seemed to dwarf the house. His presence was overwhelming, oxygen consuming. Erin couldn't take in enough precious air and found herself gulping, trying to fill her constricted lungs.

"Bart, how . . . ? Why . . . ?" She couldn't form a coherent sentence.

"Honey, I'm a little put out with you. Why didn't you tell me the mess your brother was tangled up in? Hell, I'm a good troubleshooter. Maybe I could have helped. I read about the whole thing in the Houston paper yesterday. The name just seemed to jump out at me. I tied up a few pressing business matters and then had Jim fly me out here late last night."

She knew that Ken's death had precipitated the story of the embezzlement to come out. It had been picked up by the national news services. Something that unusual couldn't be kept quiet forever. Of course Bart, who perused several newspapers each day, would have seen the story and remembered her brother's name. He had wasted no time having his pilot fly his Lear jet to San Francisco.

"Why didn't you let me know about this and help you, sugar?"

"I just didn't," Erin said sharply. When she saw his wounded look, she softened toward him. None of this was his fault. "I'm sorry, Bart. I didn't mean to snap at you. The last few days have been very trying."

"I know, baby. But I'm here now. You don't have to worry about a thing." He put a heavy arm around her shoulder and drew her close to him. He pressed her head against his chest in a comforting gesture and patted the dark curls. "I sure have missed you." His voice had taken on a quality that Erin recognized.

She fought down the sudden repulsion that gripped her. But when he tilted her head back with a finger under her chin, she didn't resist. This wasn't the time or the place to tell him that it was over between them, that she was in love with someone else.

His kiss that started with almost paternal tenderness, deepened and became possessive. She was encompassed in his arms and held against his bulk. It wasn't that Bart was fat. But his muscles weren't honed down to a wiry steeliness. He didn't have that sinewy strength and leanness of a . . . runner. Of Lance. No one looked or felt like Lance.

Lance. Lance. She had to tell Bart about Lance. Couldn't he taste Lance on her lips? Didn't he discern by her reluctant lips that she wanted to be kissing someone else?

She was gasping for air when Bart finally released her. "I've been waiting for a week for that," he said happily.

Someone behind them cleared his throat, and Erin whirled around to see Lance leaning negligently in the doorway. His casual pose was deceptive. His blue eyes reflected a glacial sheen and his chin was tilted with the arrogance that had characterized him the first day she met him. His jaw resembled an iron trap clamped shut.

"Aren't you going to introduce me to your . . . friend, Miss O'Shea?" he drawled.

She tried to catch his eyes, to plead with him for understanding and patience, but he ignored her. His eyes were riveted on Bart.

"Uh . . . Bart Stanton, this is Lance Barrett with the Treasury Department. Lance was in charge of Ken's case."

"Pleasure, Mr. Barrett," Bart said heartily and crossed the distance between them to pump Lance's hand with his usual exuberance.

"Stanton," Lance said curtly.

Bart must have noticed the rebuff, for he withdrew his hand and slanted a shrewd, if puzzled, glance at Lance. "There was an unusual turn of events in this case, wasn't there, Mr. Barrett?" Bart asked him conversationally. "Are all your cases this interesting?"

"No. This one was particularly . . . stimulat-

ing.'' Lance leveled a sardonic gaze on Erin, who
blushed to the roots of her hair. His choice of words
left their interpretation wide open for speculation.

In self-defense she cried out, ''I wish both of you
would stop referring to my brother as a 'case'! He's
dead.'' She buried her face in her hands to hide the
hurt she felt over Lance's harsh and cruel words.
Why was he behaving like this? A cold stone
seemed to have replaced the heart that had beat
against her breasts with strong passion.

Bart embraced her again. ''I'm sorry, sweetheart.
You're right.'' He patted her shoulder solicitously.
''I'd like to meet your sister-in-law. Melanie? Is
that it?''

Erin raised her head in sudden desperation. ''She
. . . she's not here. She left last night after the
funeral.''

''Left? What do you mean? She just left you here
alone?''

Erin darted a panicked, beseeching glance at
Lance. ''Yes.'' When she saw that Bart was about
to speak again, she interrupted hurriedly. ''Her parents are horrible people, Bart. She wanted to get
away from them for a while. I didn't blame her for
leaving.''

''Well, I wish I'd known you were here alone. I
would have come on over late last night when we
first got in.''

Her knees went weak with the thought of Bart
arriving while she and Lance were lying naked in

each other's arms in front of the fireplace. She gripped the edge of the hall table for support.

"I kept an eye on her, Mr. Stanton," Lance said laconically. "I was up most of the night myself."

The double entendre was so blatant that Erin didn't think Bart could help but catch it. She closed her eyes in mortification.

Apparently Bart hadn't heard Lance's suggestive words with a guilty ear as she had. He was saying, "Sugar, you look plumb tuckered out. Are you sure you're okay?"

She opened her eyes to see him leaning over her with concern stamped across his weather-creased face. "Yes," she stammered shakily. "I'm just a little tired."

"Now that Melanie is gone, there's no reason for you to stick around, is there?" he questioned her softly.

She looked at Lance, whose composed, insouciant posture hadn't changed. Yet she noticed that the muscles of his body were bunched with tension. Raising her eyes to his, she searched them deeply for some sign of the tenderness she had read in them before. There was none. They were cold and impersonal and as impenetrable as a metal shield between them.

She couldn't leave now! She had to know what he was thinking. Last night had been heaven to both of them. It had to have been as earth-moving to him as it had been to her. He couldn't have pretended that convincingly. If she left now, she would never know.

"Bart, I—" she started.

"Where's your ring?"

Bart had taken her hand and noticed immediately the absence of the large diamond ring. Erin looked up at him wordlessly, grasping for an answer. It came from another source.

"She took it off because of me."

She and Bart turned their heads in unison and stared at Lance. He was looking directly at Erin. Was he going to tell Bart about them? Yes! It would be cruel, but it would be clean. He was going to declare his love for her openly. Her heart burst with gratitude.

But as she studied him expectantly, she noticed that the eyes fixed on hers weren't warm and soft with love, but cold with . . . what? Challenge? He waited for a long while before his lips curled with disdain, then he looked at Bart. "Since we didn't know at first all the ramifications of Mr. Lyman's crime, I thought it best that the ladies not wear such valuable jewelry. I requested that Miss O'Shea take off the ring for her own protection."

It was an outrageous lie, but Bart seemed to consider the prevarication feasible. "Oh, I see. Thank you, Mr. Barrett." He turned to face Erin who, in her frozen state, looked like a pillar of salt. "How long will it take you to pack your things?"

She looked at Lance once again, but he was staring at the floor beneath his shiny shoes. He wasn't prepared to tell Bart anything. His only intention was to hurl veiled insults at her that mocked Bart, to make her feel humiliated and ashamed over what she had done out of love. His derision announced her betrayal of Bart like blaring trumpets in her head.

Lance raised his head then and looked at her. Her heart twisted with pain as she met the implacable eyes that told her clearly their shared intimacies had meant nothing more to him than a diversion.

She hung her head and mumbled, "I won't be long," as she climbed the stairs with leaden legs.

She never remembered packing her bags and checking the guest bedroom for articles left behind. She did recall retrieving her ring from the jewelry case and slipping it on her finger. She hadn't changed her mind about Bart. She could never marry him, but she would tell him later. Later. Not now. The ring weighed her down like an iron collar around her neck.

Her next conscious thought caught up with her as she stood once again at the front door. Bart was saying, "I took a cab from the airport. We'll drive your rented car back and turn it in before meeting Jim."

"Yes," she said passively, not caring if she had to walk to Houston.

"Here, sugar, let me put these in the car for you."

He went down the concrete steps with her bags, and she was left alone with Lance and Mike in the entrance hall.

"Good-bye, Mike," she said, realizing that she had never known his last name.

"Miss O'Shea." He inclined his head in a brief nod.

Lance came toward her with sauntering grace. He took her hand. His lip was lifted at one corner in a knowing smirk. "Miss O'Shea, I can't tell you what a pleasure it has been . . . knowing you." His eyes sought out the intimate places of her body that his hands and lips had learned so well.

It was the height of insults and she jerked her hand away from his. She glared at him with pure venom before she spun on her heel and marched out the door to the waiting car.

Lance didn't shut the door right away. He watched until the white Mercedes had disappeared around the corner. Then he collapsed against the wall. His anguished cry came straight from the pit of hell. "God, no, please. No! How can I stand it?"

Mike saw the blue eyes squeezed shut in an expression of incredible agony, the bared teeth, and the balled fists raised to vein-rippled temples. He mistakenly thought his boss was referring to the arrival of Mrs. Lyman's parents, who were imperiously making their way toward the front door.

The light on the intercom lit up, and the buzzer sounded. Picking up the receiver, Erin said, "Yes, Betty?"

"That gal from the Boutique Four in Tulsa is on

the line again. This is the fourth time this week she's called asking about the possibility of a trunk show with Bill Blass's holiday line.''

Erin rubbed her throbbing forehead in agitation. ''Then for the fourth time this week tell her that Mr. Blass is in Europe and I can't talk to him about it until he gets back.''

She was immediately sorry for her nasty retort and, taking a deep breath, said, ''I'm sorry, Betty.''

''No need to apologize. Don't you feel well today?''

''A little weary,'' she admitted.

''Why don't you lie down for a while?''

''No. I have too much to do.''

''Okay,'' Betty said without conviction. ''While I've got you on the line, Lester called and begged that he be able to take someone with him to the show at Walsh's in Albuquerque. It's an overnight trip and he says he'll kill himself if he can't take his live-in along.''

Lester was one of the male models that Erin frequently used in her style shows. ''Is the live-in male or female?''

Betty said, chuckling, ''You know Lester.''

''Then tell him he'll just have to kill himself. The Walshes are very conservative and very straight and very rich, and I need to hold on to that account. We can't jeopardize it. The live-in, male or female, stays at home.''

''I'd already told him to load the pistol, but I promised to ask.''

Erin laughed, silently thanking Betty for injecting a little levity into this depressing day. "Thanks, Betty, you're a real friend."

"You bet I am. Excuse me now. I have to get back to that broad in Tulsa. If you need anything, holler." She clicked off her line and Erin leaned back in her deep leather chair.

The yielding cushions suffocated her, however, and she stood up and walked to the window. She stared out at the Houston skyline, bathed in a hot, watery glare from a humid sky. This was a terrible climate to be in during July. The heat was oppressive, the humidity was cloying, and the air was thick. One couldn't breathe.

Especially if she were five months pregnant.

Unconsciously Erin rubbed her hand over her stomach which was still flat by most standards. Never having had any tummy at all, she felt like it was enormous. She could still fit into most of her regular clothes, but she had preferred to start wearing loose-fitting dresses.

As to everything these days, she was apathetic to her lovely surroundings. Her office was decorated in ivory, teal, and peach. The gracious setting, decorated in such good taste, was intended to impress clients, which it never failed to do.

Ironically, today her dress matched her decor. It was a soft voile print that picked up the colors of the room. Albert Nipon hadn't intended it to be a maternity dress, but it served that purpose. It buttoned down one side, over the breast. The bodice was pleated and fell into a graceful skirt beyond where a waistline would be.

The pregnancy had cost her very little discomfort, she conceded. There was always that annoying feeling of being stuffed full even when she was hungry. The doctor said that was because she was normally so thin. She had suffered through a few weeks of morning sickness, but a tiny yellow tablet before breakfast had helped. She was very cautious now about the medication she took. Ever since San . . .

It mattered not how it got there, her mind always came back to that. To San Francisco. To Lance Barrett. To the hateful and cruelly amused expression he wore that last time she had seen him before she left with Bart.

Bart. Dear Bart. Why must he have been hurt? She could remember the day she had quietly returned the ostentatious engagement ring to him.

"What's this?" he had asked, staring down at the ring stupidly.

"I can't marry you, Bart," she said simply.

He had shaken his large, burly head as if to clear it. "What do you mean, Erin? Why?"

"Because I'm pregnant."

He had stared at her through uncomprehending eyes. She could have been speaking a language he didn't understand. Finally he blinked and closed his mouth, which was hanging slack. "Pregnant?" he asked.

"Yes."

She watched as his stupefaction gradually turned

to understanding, then changed to anger. "Pregnant!?" This time the word was a shouted accusation. "How? Who?" Before she could form an explanation, he demanded, "Answer me, damn you."

She met his accusing eyes calmly. Her hands, clasped tightly in her lap, were the only concession to the trembling fear she felt for this bear whose ire had been raised. "It doesn't matter, Bart. The baby is mine. No one else's."

"Don't play coy with me, you bitch. It takes two to make a baby. Even this ol' redneck, who you must think is really dense, knows that." He gripped her arms hard. "Who was the man, because, by God, I know it wasn't me! And it wasn't for lack of trying!"

"Bart, please," she begged, "you're hurting me."

He looked down at the white knuckles of his hands that gripped her delicate arms. "I'm sorry," he muttered. He released her immediately and stood up. He paced the length of the sofa in her living room several times before he stopped in front of her and said, "It was Barrett, wasn't it?"

Her eyes flew to him in surprise. How had he known? It was useless to lie. "Yes," she said quietly.

"Dammit!" he cursed, slamming his meaty fist into the palm of his hand. "I'll kill that bastard. Did he rape you? If he hurt you—"

She shook her head vehemently. "No. It wasn't rape."

Her denial doused his impetus. Quieter, more calmly, he asked hopefully, pathetically, "Did he seduce you, sugar? You couldn't help yourself. Is that it, honey?"

Tears streamed down her face, but she looked up at him and answered honestly, "No, Bart. I knew exactly what I was doing."

The massive shoulders slumped in rejection and dejection. He put his hands in his pockets. "I see," was all he said. They were quiet for long moments. Erin cried softly.

"I guess the sonofabitch refuses to marry you. Worthless scum. You say the word, Erin, and I'll have Mr. Barrett taken care of. I know the people to call. He'll be snuffed out so quick—"

Erin catapulted off the couch and grasped him by the shoulders, shaking him frantically. Her face was wet with tears. "No!" she shrieked. "No. Don't you dare hurt him. Say you won't. God! He's not to be hurt." She collapsed against him as Bart put protective arms around her and patted her on the back.

Soothingly he said, "Shhh. Honey, calm down. I'm not going to do anything you don't want me to." With a certain fear in his voice he asked, "Are you okay now?" Bart Stanton, the terror of boardrooms, was intimidated by no one or nothing. But an hysterical woman reduced him to mush.

She pushed away from him and nodded. "Yes," she sniffed. Raising swimming eyes, she said, "Bart, he doesn't even know. Promise me you won't tell him or hurt him in any way."

He looked at her with that shrewd scrutiny that had earned him his reputation. "So that's the way it is," he said slowly. "You love him, don't you?"

"Yes," she said without shyness or hesitation.

He went to the window and stared out at her tree-shaded lawn. A panoply of early spring spread out before him. Everything was lush and green, verdant, fecund. The thought sickened him as he said, "I know how you feel about your religion and all, but maybe it would be better, all things considered, if you had an . . . uh . . . operation."

She smiled at his cowardice over saying a word. She shook her head with a sad little smile. "No, Bart. It's not just because of my religion. It's me. I could never do that."

"You won't give it up for adoption." It wasn't a question. He already knew that answer.

"Do you really think, knowing my background, that I would even consider such a thing?" she admonished him kindly. "No, Bart. I'll rear my baby by myself."

He came back to her quickly. He spoke hurriedly as if he might change his mind before the words were out. "Sweetheart, marry me. I don't care about the baby. I didn't mean those things I said. I was angry, honey. I've wanted you for so long. I swear it doesn't matter. Hell, everybody'll think the baby is mine anyway."

"But we would know different, wouldn't we?" she asked gently. "I don't want to live a lie like that, Bart. And I don't want you to have to either."

"I love you. I want you on any terms."

She sighed and ran her fingers through his thick, dark hair. "I know. But my answer is still no."

She had refused him and continued to do so. Bart wasn't as persistent as he had been the first time he asked her to marry him, but he remained close at hand as if hoping she'd change her mind.

But she wouldn't. She touched her stomach again lovingly just as the buzzer on her intercom sounded again and distracted her from her daydreaming.

"Yes, Betty?" she asked, pressing down the button on the panel.

"There is someone here to see you, Erin. Are you free?"

"Yes. Who is it?"

"A Mr. Lance Barrett."

CHAPTER
Twelve

Her heart skidded to a jolting stop. Respiration was impossible. Her eyes closed against a wave of dizziness that almost made her fall to the thick carpet. The world slipped off its axis and tilted crazily before righting itself. She managed to grip the edge of the desk and ease down into her chair.

"Erin, did you hear me?" Betty asked.

"Y . . . yes." What could she do? Lance was here. Just beyond that door. She had to see him. But how could she bear it?

What did he want? What if he realized her condition? What could she tell him? The questions tumbled through her mind, but there were no answers. She would have to brazen it out and hope for the best.

"Send him in, Betty," she answered with a modicum of poise she was far from feeling.

She ran an anxious hand over her hair, licked her

lips, and smoothed the bodice of her dress over her breasts, swollen with pregnancy. He mustn't see. His perception was so keen. His training was to see things—

He walked through the double oak door.

If she thought that her memory of him had magnified his physical attributes, she was wrong. He was even more handsome and virile than she remembered. His hair was casual, a trifle longer, and bleached lighter from the summer sun.

The blue eyes had lost none of their brilliance, though the lightened eyebrows were a stark contrast to his tanned face. There were fine white lines fanning out from the corners of his eyes that she didn't remember, but they were probably only more noticeable because of his tanned complexion.

If anything, the cleft in his chin lent itself to more arrogance. As he smiled at her, however, she noticed a vulnerability around his stern mouth that hadn't been there last February.

The most drastic difference in his appearance was his clothes. She had teased him about wearing a uniform of dark suits, white shirts, and dark ties. He had defended himself by saying that government agents shouldn't attract attention by wearing designer sport coats and flashy shirts.

His light yellow shirt wasn't flashy, but the cut of his dark brown coat was surely European. The tan trousers fit his thighs and hips in a way that denoted they had been tailor made. There was no necktie around his neck. Instead his collar was left open to reveal a peek at that tawny mat of hair that covered his torso.

Her resolve to remain cool and impersonal was vaporized when he seemed to invade this feminine domain with the masculine force of a rampaging vandal. She fell victim.

"Hello, Erin," he said.

She should stand and walk toward him and take his hand, but she was afraid to leave her hiding place behind the desk. If she stood, he might detect her pregnancy.

"Hello, Lance," she returned warmly. Her lips were quivering, but she was determined to appear cordial, as if greeting an old friend. "Come in and sit down." She indicated the chair in front of her desk. "This is a surprise."

He was just as aloof as she as he crossed the room, taking in the environs of the office with those penetrating eyes. There was no escaping them. She would stick to her wise decision and stay seated behind the desk.

"This is very nice, Erin," he said, indicating the office with a sweeping gesture of his hand. "I'm impressed."

He smiled at her as he took his seat, and her heart did an erratic dance. His teeth flashed whitely against his dark skin. He was devastating.

"Thank you. This isn't our busiest time of year. Things slow down in the summer. We won't be really active again until our clients start having fashion shows in the fall for the Christmas season." She would be very pregnant by then. How would she manage that hectic pace?

"I probably should have called before I came, but I thought it would be better to see you in person."

His words were almost verbatim what she had said to him when she arrived at the Lyman residence. He looked up at her. Did she remember? She did. They smiled at each other.

"You were right. I'm glad you came straight here," she parroted what his response had been. Then they both laughed self-consciously. For a moment there was a tense silence as they looked at each other. Lance unbuttoned his coat and that triggered Erin's next comment. "You look different."

"How?"

"Your clothes. They're not as . . . conservative as what you wore before."

He had noticed her pause and smiled that sardonic smile that she well remembered. "You mean not as *dull*, don't you?"

She laughed and admitted, "Yes, dull. Has the Treasury Department issued new uniforms?"

He shrugged and, watching her reaction to his words, said, "I don't know. I don't work for it anymore."

She was stunned. "What?" Her eyes were wide with unasked questions.

"I resigned a while back. Actually I'm here today on my last official duty. I've gone into business for myself with another guy."

"Lance . . ." she groped for words. "I don't

know what to say. Are you happy? Is that what you want? You were so good at your work.''

"Thank you." He smiled. "I'm using my past experience for what I'm doing now. This friend of mine quit the department several years ago and started his own company. He goes into banks, businesses, whatever, and holds seminars on how to prevent and detect internal white-collar crimes. He also trains employees of said businesses on how to handle a criminal, like during a robbery or something."

He raised the ankle of one foot to his opposite knee. "Anyway, he called me a few months ago. His business has gotten out of hand. He couldn't handle all his clients and wanted to know if I'd be interested in joining him. It had been a while since he'd been out in the field and could use some of my expertise to update his material."

He dropped his leg back to the floor and leaned forward, emphasizing his next words. "Erin, I'm amazed at how lucrative this business is. Corporations are willing to pay us a tremendous amount of money in order to save themselves much more. We're making a lot of money and providing a valuable service at the same time."

His enthusiasm was contagious and Erin was happy for his success. He was so much more relaxed, less wary, than she had ever seen him.

"To tell you the truth," he said, "I grew disenchanted with my work after . . . San Francisco." His voice had lowered in pitch and volume with his last two words and his eyes pierced through her from under the golden eyebrows.

It had been five months, yet any reference to Ken still brought a lump to Erin's throat. His death before she could ever meet him was still a wound that opened frequently. She murmured, "I think I can understand that."

"Do you hear often from Mrs. Lyman?"

Erin's face brightened considerably. "Yes, Melanie moved to Oregon and got a job with a florist, which is a natural for her. I get frequent letters. She sold the house in San Francisco and loves her work and small apartment. Last week she called me, and I'm convinced she'll be happy." Erin was smiling mysteriously.

"Why?" he asked with a curious grin on his face. He was really interested.

"Well, as it happens there is a Mr. Alan Carter who owns a nursery that sells plants to the florist. He is a 'sweet, nice man in his late twenties.' "

They both laughed over Melanie's description. "He was widowed when his wife was suddenly and tragically killed a year and a half ago, and he was left with a two-year-old son."

"Aha!" said Lance.

"Melanie called last week to ask me if I thought it was too soon after Ken's death for her to go to dinner with Mr. Carter. 'Of course, it won't really be a *date*. Just two lonely people having dinner together. And his little boy, who is so *precious*, will come, too.' I think that's an exact quote."

"She's a terrific lady. I hope she's happy," Lance said seriously.

"I think Mr. Carter, or someone like him, is just what she needs. I'm only thankful that she's not in San Francisco with her parents."

"Amen to that."

Silence stretched between them again. They avoided looking at each other, though their awareness hadn't diminished at all. In fact they were captivated with each other. Every gesture was noted. Each breath was cataloged. The tiniest inflection of voice was heard. The air was redolent with tension.

He had said he was on his last official duty for the Department of the Treasury. Partially out of curiosity and partially out of a need to break the palpable silence, Erin asked, "Why did you come to see me? Has it something to do with Ken? You said it was official."

"Yes. I have something for you." Reaching into the breast pocket of his jacket he stood up. "Why don't you come over here?" He was walking toward the pastel sofa near the wide picture window. He apparently expected her to follow him.

She would have to stand up and expose herself to his uncanny perception. But refusing to budge would only draw more attention to her, and that was to be avoided. Sucking in her breath to flatten her stomach as much as possible, she stood up on unsteady knees.

With trepidation that at any moment he was going

to realize her condition, she crossed to the sofa where he was waiting. Only after she sat down did he take a seat at the opposite end.

"Erin, I've had this for several months." He indicated an ordinary white, letter-sized envelope. "Before Mrs. Lyman sold her house, she sorted through drawers and files. Anything she thought I might use to complete my report, she sent to me in Washington."

He paused and looked deeply into her brown eyes. "I don't think she intended to send this. She probably didn't even know it was in with the other papers and documents. I guess I should have sent it back to her, but I knew you would want to have it, and I think she would want you to."

Her curiosity knew no bounds. If his intention was to pique her interest, he had succeeded. He handed her the envelope. It was several seconds before her eyes dropped from his and looked down at what she held in her hand.

She lifted the flap and reached inside. Her fingers closed around the edges of a stiff piece of paper. Taking it out she saw that it was a black and white photograph, yellowed with age. Her heart began to pound and there was a roaring in her ears as her throat went dry.

From the clothes that the three people in the picture wore, she could tell that the time period captured was about thirty years ago.

A young woman sat on a stone bench in a surrounding that looked like a city park. Standing shyly next to her knee was a small boy, still a toddler. On her lap she held a baby. Round, dark eyes looked out from behind a lacy bonnet on the infant's head.

The woman stared directly into the camera, but she wasn't smiling. It was as if she didn't really see the photographer. Her mind seemed to be far away. Her eyes were sad, but very much like those of the young boy and the baby. Her features were delicate, almost fragile, as though she had a tenuous hold on her life. Her impermanence was evident in the way she held her head, in the way she clutched the baby to her, and the tender hand she rested on the small boy's shoulder. She seemed to bespeak a certain desperation. Only the softness of her features revealed her resignation to whatever tragedy had beset her.

Tears had long since blinded Erin's eyes, yet she continued to stare down at the photograph. The minutes ticked by as she assimilated every detail of the picture, trying to pierce the flat surface and see into the third dimension, into the woman's mind. Lance didn't interrupt. He didn't move. He scarcely breathed.

Finally, she looked up at him. God, she was beautiful, he thought. Even though her face was wet with tears, she was the most gorgeous woman he had ever seen. It had taken almost more nerve than he could muster to walk through the door to this office. The last time he had seen her, she was throwing poison darts at him with those dark eyes. A rational man would have retreated from where he wasn't wanted and left well enough alone.

But not him. Not Lance Barrett. No. He was a glutton for punishment. He had to see her one more time. He had to convince himself that what happened in San Francisco was only a fleeting fancy. Affairs like that were doomed to be short-lived. Too hot not to cool down. Wasn't that how the song went? He'd see her and then he could banish her ghost forever from his haunted mind.

But he knew it wouldn't be that way, and it wasn't. Something had happened to him last February and he hadn't been the same since. He had fallen in love.

He argued that he was too old to be acting like such a damn fool over a woman. He snapped at his men for the least petty aggravation, venting his short temper on them. One had awakened with a cracked jaw after suggesting that a toss with a winsome wench might improve Lance's irascibility. He couldn't sleep, couldn't eat. His family and friends grew to despise him. But no more than he despised himself.

Erin had once commissioned him to hell. Well, he had been, and he didn't like it. The only bit of heaven he had glimpsed for the last five months was the sight of her face as he walked through the door of this office.

Dammit! He was worse off now than ever before.

He was quaking inside from being this near her, wanting to proclaim his love, yet not daring to.

She smelled delicious. Her complexion glowed from some inner source. Her lips were moist and parted. He could see her dainty pink tongue resting behind the row of perfect white teeth. God, he wanted to feel it against his lips, in his mouth, taste her.

Looking up at him now with those tear-flooded eyes, it took all his control to keep from crushing her against him and never letting go. She was different and yet painfully familiar. She was the woman who had loved him so completely, fit him so uniquely. She was Erin O'Shea. His Erin.

But there was something . . .

"There's an inscription on the back," he told her gently.

Turning the picture over, Erin read aloud, " 'Ken's mother, Mary Margaret Conway, and his sister. Died two weeks after picture taken of tuberculosis. Little girl already adopted when we got Ken. God bless them.' " It was dated and signed MRL.

"Those were Ken's adoptive mother's initials. My guess is that she got the photograph when she adopted Ken. I found it in a manila folder marked in Ken's handwriting as 'Mother's papers.' He probably didn't get this until after she died."

"Then he knew about me."

"I suppose so."

The tears were flowing again. "Lance, this is my mother," she whispered, smoothing her fingers across the face in the picture. "Mary Margaret Conway. I know her name."

"And she loved you. She probably knew that she was about to die and took you to the orphanage to see that you were taken care of."

"My father?" She looked up at him expectantly.

He only shook his head sadly. "I don't know, Erin. But now you have a name. That's a lead if you want to start from there."

She sighed, but it wasn't out of sadness. It stemmed from a sense of peace and well-being. "I don't know. Maybe sometime. For right now, this is enough. More than enough. I . . ." She choked on the emotion clogging her throat. "I don't know how to thank you." Slowly she raised her eyes to his. She saw a strange shine glossing over the blue irises.

"It was the least I could do, Erin. I felt responsible for your losing your brother. When I saw this, I wanted to bring it to you. I don't think Mrs. Lyman will mind."

Imperceptibly they moved closer together. Each was caught up in a maelstrom of whirling emotions. His clean, masculine scent filled her head and numbed her brain. His hard, strong body promised solace for someone who wanted and needed support. Someone who was troubled by problems that seemed insoluble. Someone whose heart had been shattered five months ago and still continued to be chiseled away a little each day.

"Erin," he said gruffly. "Erin—"

The door was flung open and Bart barreled into the room. "Sugar, are you okay?" He glanced quickly to Erin before glaring at Lance, who had flown off the sofa and stood facing Bart dangerously. "What in the hell are you doing here?" Bart demanded.

"None of your damn business," Lance said with a deadly calm.

"Like hell it's not," Bart challenged. "I ought to pound the everlovin' crap out of you."

"You might try," Lance said placidly.

Erin remained on the sofa, too overwrought to stand and fight them both. Her head was splitting and her mouth had a sour taste in it. "Please, please. Both of you."

"Has he upset you, honey? You've been crying." Bart folded his immense bulk into the ludicrous facsimile of a squat in front of the sofa and covered Erin's cold hands with his.

"No, he—" Erin began.

"What I had to see Erin about was private and no concern of yours, Stanton," Lance barked.

"Everything about her concerns me," Bart declared, standing up to his full height.

"Not what she and I say to each other." Erin knew that tone of Lance's. He was furious, and the cold, brittle voice rained on them like shards of glass. His eyes were frigid as they locked with Bart's.

Bart was no coward, but he recognized a worthy opponent. He backed away slightly. "Then we'll leave it up to her." He took his eyes off Lance for only a split second to look down at Erin. "Sugar, do you have anything more to say to Mr. Barrett?"

The import of the question wasn't lost on her. She knew what he was asking. *Did she want to tell Lance about their baby?* God, what was she to do?

She wanted to tell him. To see a glow of happiness and love replace that fearsome glint in his eyes would be the most beautiful sight in the world.

But dare she take the risk? What if he looked at her with disgust? Suppose he berated her for not practicing birth control? Could she bear a patronizing attitude born of guilt and a sense of responsibility? Would he feel obligated to do the "right thing" by her?

Don't ever be afraid of me, Erin. Never . . .

No. She couldn't trap him by announcing her pregnancy. As much as she wanted him, she wouldn't take him on those terms. Scheming women had used that resource since history began. It was the ultimate weapon to assure victory—the trump card.

She loved Lance. That was an undeniable fact. But he had never expressed love for her. In all those passion-laden hours they had shared in San Francisco, he had never made any allusions to loving her.

Perfect, perfect . . . I'll wait . . .

Her appeal to him was strictly physical. True, it was consuming. But to Erin, who had always wanted the strong bonds of a family based on love, it wasn't enough.

I don't know what's happening to me . . .

Looking up at him, she fell under the full power of his eyes. They seemed to touch her soul and ignite her spirit. She looked at him deep and long, for she knew that this might be the last time. It might have to last her for the rest of her life.

You have two very feminine habits, Erin O'Shea . . .

Finally, she lowered her eyes and shook her head. "No. I have nothing more to say."

There was a heavy silence in the room so complete that they could hear the traffic several stories below them on the Houston streets. She closed her eyes against the pain in her heart when she heard Lance turn on his heels and stalk to the door. The clicking sound of the closing latch was like a bullet that ended her life.

She collapsed on the sofa, succumbing to her misery. The spasm of heartbreak lasted for so long that Bart became genuinely concerned for her health. He tried in his endearing, clumsy way to comfort her, but was unsuccessful. Finally, his desperation bordered on anger and he commanded, "Look here, Erin, I don't want you to lose that baby of yours, so straighten up!"

More than what he said, it was his use of her

name that caused her to sit up and choke back lingering tears.

"That's more like it," he grumbled.

"You called me by my name, Bart."

"Don't I always?" he asked with a puzzled expression.

She smiled and fondly touched his cheek. "No," she whispered.

He stood up and took a few steps away from her. "Sugar, this is the hardest thing I've ever had to say, but here goes. You should tell Barrett about the baby. The way he looked at you, for a minute there, I thought, well . . . it was like . . . you know. Like he might love you. Let me go after him."

"No, Bart. I can't tell him."

Quietly, hesitantly he said, "He has a right to know, darlin'. That baby is his too, you know."

She sighed. She had thought of that. "Yes. He'll have to know, of course, but not now. Maybe when the baby's born, my lawyers or something . . ." Her voice trailed off. She had no energy left.

"You know I still want to marry you." Bart cleared his throat. "Will you change your mind? I love you." An incredible sadness clouded his dark eyes.

"I love you too, Bart. You're the dearest friend I have," she said sincerely.

"Yeah, I know," he snorted mirthlessly. After a moment he asked, "Do you want me to call the doctor and have him send out a tranquilizer? Frankly, you look like hell," he said.

She laughed ruefully. "Well, in this case looks aren't deceiving because that's just how I feel." When the crease between his brows deepened, she said, "No, I don't need a tranquilizer. It's been an eventful day. I just want to go home to bed."

"Can I drive you?"

"No. I'll be fine."

As they walked toward the door, Bart asked, "Why did Barrett come here in the first place?"

Erin's fingers closed around the envelope that contained the picture so precious to her. It was the only remnant she had of her mother and brother. It was also the only thing that Lance had ever given her. For a while, she wanted to keep it to herself.

"It was only some unfinished business about Ken," she answered vaguely.

Erin was drained from the heat and exhausted from the emotional upheaval of the day as she let herself in the back door of her house. She noticed that the petunias in the flower beds were drooping with thirst. If she had any conscience, she would come out here and water them, but she doubted that she could amass the energy tonight.

She switched on the central air conditioning system that had been one of her improvements to the house. Laboriously climbing the stairs, she went into her bedroom and turned on the overhead fan to stir the sultry air until the air conditioner could take over.

She changed into a full, loose sundress that was

held on to her shoulders with thin straps. The pale blue gauzy fabric swirled around her like a cloud. No longer able to tolerate any confinement, she peeled off her panty hose and slipped on a pair of bikini panties, discarding her other underwear.

The thought of food was obnoxious, but she went downstairs into the kitchen and fixed a glass of iced tea, liberally spiking it with lemon juice.

Walking into her living room, she paused as usual and enjoyed the sight of it. She loved this room. The walls were painted a dark beige which contrasted nicely with the white woodwork and shutters. The sofa and easy chairs were also white, but were heaped with pillows in vivid shades of blue, green, and orange. As if on command, her eyes strayed to the white brick fireplace. It was one of three in the house.

Lance had lit a fire in that unused fireplace that night. What was on his mind when he did that? Had he been thinking of her? Had he wished she would come down—

Stop it!

She sank down in one of the easy chairs and put her feet up on an ottoman. In her hand was the photograph Lance had delivered to her today. As she sipped her tea, she stared at the picture of her family. Tomorrow she would buy a gold frame to put it in. What kind did she want? Something Victorian with filigreeing around the edges? Or something simple so as not to detract from the photograph itself?

For the first time in her life, she felt like she had a heritage. She could be content.

Almost. If it weren't for the heartache over the man—

She groaned when the doorbell sounded. It was probably the paper boy collecting for this month. With weary limbs, she got up from the chair and dragged herself to the front door.

Lance was standing on the porch between the urns of red geraniums on either side of the door. He had forsaken the brown coat and there was one more button on his shirt undone. The sleeves were rolled to his elbows.

She shrank from the livid anger on his face.

"Take off your clothes."

She stared at him dumbfounded. Her ears must be playing tricks on her. "What—"

"I said to take off your clothes." He barged past her into the living room. "And if you don't, I will." She shut the door and turned to face him. His voice brooked no argument, and she didn't doubt for one moment he'd do what he threatened.

Well, she wasn't going to cringe against the door in fear. She pushed away from that false sanctuary and lifted her chin defensively. "You'd have to kill me first."

"Don't tempt me," he growled. "I'm on the verge now of wringing your lovely neck."

"What have I done to provoke you?" Her heart was racing. Did he know? Of course he did. He never missed anything.

His eyes narrowed on her. The golden-flecked lashes formed a thick brush over them. "I couldn't quite figure out what it was while I was with you, but I knew that something was different. I was just about to board the airplane when it finally hit me." His face suddenly lost its belligerence. If he had stripped away a mask, the change in his expression couldn't have been more disparate. "Erin—"

He didn't finish. Instead he walked toward her and reached out to touch her. Reflexively, she protected her stomach with her hands. Inexorably, he moved her hands aside and settled his palms against her.

The abdomen that he knew as almost concave and supple was now turgid and slightly convex. He inclined toward her, keeping his hands as they were, and released a long, ragged breath. She saw a look that resembled pain in his eyes as he asked, "Stanton?"

Her lips trembled when she tried to smile. "No, Lance."

The blue eyes asked that monumental question and hers answered by closing briefly in affirmation.

Slowly, almost fearfully, he gathered her into his arms and continued squeezing until they were like one unit. He pressed his forehead against hers. "God, Erin, why didn't you tell me? Were you just going to have my baby and never let me know about it? *Why?*"

She had never heard such confusion in Lance's voice. Bewilderment was written on every feature of his handsome face. He wasn't invincible. He was a man.

She hugged him tight. "Don't you think I wanted to? But how could I? That's not something you write a man in a letter, tell him over the telephone. For all I knew, I'd never see you again. I was going to let you know after the baby was born, but until then I couldn't take the chance."

"Chance?" he asked, pushing away from her, but holding on to her shoulders. "What kind of chance?"

She averted her eyes from his severe probing. "Lance, I didn't know how you'd react to the . . . the baby. You might have wanted me to . . ." He grasped her unspoken meaning.

"And you couldn't do that." It wasn't a question.

"No!" she exclaimed.

"Why?"

She licked her lips nervously. "B—because my religion doesn't condone it."

"No other reason?"

"Yes, me. I don't think I could ever do something like that."

"Is there anything else that kept you from aborting my baby?" His tenacious grip on her shoulders indicated his urgency.

"No," she answered safely. He didn't believe her.

"Yes, there is, Erin. Tell me."

"No."

"Tell me, dammit!" he shouted.

"Because I love you!" she shouted back.

The words bounced off the walls of the still house as the two people, breathing agitatedly, stared at each other.

Then she was crushed against him. One arm held her like an iron band across her back while the fingers of his other hand buried themselves in her short dark curls and pressed her head into his chest. She could feel his lips moving in her hair.

"Erin, Erin, do you know the hell we've put each other through? To think you were alone all this time when I should have been here with you. I wanted to be. God, how I wanted to be, baby or not."

She wrapped her arms around his waist and wished he could absorb her into his flesh. "What are you saying, Lance?"

"When you left me in San Francisco, I thought I'd die from wanting you. Loving you." He lowered his head and kissed her fervently on the neck. "But I had to let you go. When you had the chance to tell Stanton about us, you didn't. I thought you wanted to come back with him and forget about me."

"Oh, Lance. You were so sarcastic and cruel, so remote. I thought you had used me for entertainment and was glad Bart was conveniently relieving you of me."

His arms tightened around her, telling her how wrong she had been. "My hatefulness was only a defense mechanism. I fought loving you every step of the way and was afraid you'd know I'd fallen in love with you. I imagined you and Stanton having a good laugh at my expense.''

He brushed his lips across her fragrant shoulders. She pulled the shirttail out of his waistband and slipped her hands under it, kneading the muscles of his back.

"Do you remember Higgins?" he asked. "He's the guy here in Houston I had check up on you that first day. I've had him keeping an eye on you. I knew you hadn't married Stanton."

"Then why didn't you come to me sooner?"

"I know you probably won't understand this, but I couldn't come to you until I had something to offer."

He released her and walked toward the couch and sat down, clasping his hands between his knees. "When I met you, you were successful and far wealthier than I. I admired you for it. I'm not nearly as chauvinistic as you accused me of being, Erin." He grinned up at her, then grew serious again. "But I couldn't declare my love and propose marriage when I didn't even have a home to take you to, other than a dusty apartment in D.C. I really didn't have a future, none I'd offer you. I couldn't come to you until I was established and earning more money."

She sat down next to him and stretched her arm across his broad shoulders. "That made no difference to me. It never did. I told you that."

"Well, it made a helluva lot of difference to me."

He took her in his arms and drew a deep breath. "Will you marry me, Erin? I'm not rich like Stanton by a long shot, but I—"

She placed her fingers against his lips. "You've given me what I wanted most in the world." Taking his hand, she placed it over her stomach and smiled tremulously.

"For years now, ever since Joseph's death, I've been searching for something. I worked obsessively, thinking professional success was my goal. That wasn't it. Relentlessly I tracked down Ken, and I'm overjoyed at having known about his life with Melanie. Thanks to you, the questions that plagued me about the woman who gave me birth have been answered. I'm at peace about why she left me at the orphanage. But, Lance"—here her voice changed and cracked with emotion—"I really didn't know what I was searching for until I found you."

He kissed her then, closing his mouth over hers and delighting in that taste that had never been far from his mind. She opened her mouth to his greedy passion and matched it.

When they pulled apart, he said, "I've been looking at houses in Georgetown, but I like this one." He wasn't looking at her house. He was looking at her chest and tracing the neckline of her dress with his fingers.

She tried to suppress her sudden excitement. "Would this be . . . ? I mean, could we live here with your business?"

"All I need is a business telephone and an airport," he grinned. "When can I move in?"

She knew this might be a tremendous sacrifice for him professionally and psychologically. He was doing it for her. She loved him all the more for it. In answer to his question, she said, "When you make an honest woman out of me."

They kissed deeply again. His hand disappeared under the soft fabric of her dress and caressed her thigh.

As she nibbled his throat she asked, "Will you take me to Shreveport and meet my mother?" She raised her eyes to his in supplication. "Lance, she doesn't know about you or the baby. I didn't want to worry her until I had a reasonable resolution outlined in my mind."

"And that's all I am? A 'reasonable resolution'?" He acted offended, but he was smiling. He toyed with the lace-edged elastic leg of her panties.

"There may be a shotgun wedding when we tell her." She smiled while outlining his lips with her fingertips.

"I've never been gun-shy," he said and took her mouth in another fathomless kiss.

"My work may involve some travel for a while until I can train others to hold the seminars."

"I'll go with you," she chirped brightly.

"No, you won't. You'll stay home and take care of baby."

"Baby can go with us. I'm not going to be one

of those wives who forsakes her husband for the benefit of her children. I'll go with you.''

He started laughing, and she frowned on his amusement when she was trying to be serious. "What's so funny?"

"You. I don't know why I thought you'd grow all manageable and acquiescent after you became a wife. You'll always defy me.''

She pushed away from him. "I will not!"

He laughed harder. ''See! You're doing it now.''

"I'll show you defiance, Mr. Barrett!'' she shouted and jumped off the couch. Before he could protest, she had stomped upstairs. Moments later he heard a door slam.

''That woman is going to be the death of me,'' he muttered, raking his fingers through his hair. He stood at the bottom of the stairs and looked up. Then a broad grin broke across his face. "But I'll die happy.'' He was whipping off his shirt by the time his foot touched the bottom step.

All the doors upstairs were opened except one. It took him only a minute to do what he had to do before he flung it open. He stood framed in the door like an avenging savage. His nudity was his armor and contributed to his ferocity.

Erin, who was lying on the bed waiting for him, burst out laughing. Their minds had run the same course. She wore only her panties.

His smile was arrogant as he swaggered toward her. The mattress shifted as he placed a heavy knee along her hip and knelt beside her. "You think you're real funny, don't you?" he asked.

Her smile was impish as she rolled against him and touched him invitingly. "What do *you* think?" she taunted.

With an insolent expression on his face, he hooked his fingers under the sides of her panties and eased them down her slender legs. He had intended to continue their teasing, but when he gazed at the body enriched by motherhood, lying beside him, he couldn't.

He raised his eyes to her and said thickly, "I think you're beautiful."

He covered her completely and they marveled again at that harmonizing fit of their bodies which matched them together like pieces of a puzzle.

"How can mere human skin be this soft?" he murmured against the first rib under her arm. His lips foraged their way up her neck and then balanced just above her quivering mouth. Lips and tongues battled playfully before a fusion of their mouths left no room for concentration on anything except the commitment the kiss solemnized.

At last they were breathless, and Lance pulled away slightly to better view her body. The subtle changes in her breasts intrigued him. His caress was gentle as he touched her. "Are they sore?" he asked with concern.

She ran her finger down his long, slender nose. "Not very."

"I don't want to hurt you."

"You won't. You'll relieve me," she said, cupping the undersides of her breasts and raising them slightly.

His lips made the barest movements against the sensitive flesh. Then his tongue bathed her tender nipples with an exquisite warm wetness. She arched against him and he sought to assuage the throbbing ache in her center with stroking fingers, but it wasn't enough.

Sliding downward, he lay his head on that part of her body where his baby lay nestled and kissed it reverently. Erin entwined her fingers in the sun-bleached hair and drew him even closer. His mouth planted tiny kisses on her abdomen and nuzzled her until tenderness gave way to passion.

"Lance," she gasped when his fervent lips paid homage to that mysterious delta that safeguarded his most precious treasure.

He reveled in her essence. "Erin, Erin," he spoke against her dewy skin. "What an addictive sweetness you are."

His name was almost like a sob as it rolled off her lips. "Lance, please . . ."

He raised himself over her and settled between silken thighs. "Erin, tell me if I—"

His words were trapped in his mouth as she sealed them inside with her anxious lips. Her beseeching hands on his hips convinced him that his caution was unnecessary. He accepted what was so freely offered, moving his hands under her and lifting her to honor his total possession.

Temporarily they were sated. Their legs were entangled; stomachs were cushioned together as she lay atop his chest. Propping up on an elbow, she plucked at his chest hair. "Lance, you have another gray hair!"

He chuckled. "Since I met you, it's a wonder they're not all gray."

She buried her face in the wiry mat and kissed him. Absently he combed his fingers through her hair. "Erin, how did you feel when you found out you were pregnant? Distressed? Happy?"

She raised her head and her face was warm with love when she said, "I was thrilled, Lance. It was the most special feeling and I . . . I . . . I can't explain it. Wonderful isn't strong enough. And I was surprised. For days after I first noticed the symptoms, I couldn't imagine what was wrong with me."

Lance laughed. "Miss O'Shea, didn't you know that what we were doing so much of could make babies?"

Punishment for his impudent question was a smacking kiss on his ear. "Of course I knew it could make babies! It's just that when we . . . uh . . . while you are . . . well, it never entered my mind." She was overcome by a rash of timidity, but she managed to add, "When I'm loving you, Lance, I don't think about anything else."

Cradling her face between his palms, he stared into her ebony eyes. "Erin, *do* you love me?"

"I've already told you."

"Tell me again," he said menacingly.

They smiled, remembering the day he had bombarded her with questions in the Lymans' small paneled study. Now, as then, she answered him honestly. "I love you, Lance."

Just before he kissed her, he felt an infinitesimal fluttering against his abdomen. Erin hadn't moved. What the—?

His blue eyes widened in surprised awe as comprehension dawned. "Is that . . . ?"

Erin smiled down and lowered her lips to his. "Yes, darling. He's as eager for his daddy as I am."

More
Sandra Brown!

Please turn this page
for a
bonus excerpt from
The Silken Web
a new
Warner Books hardcover
coming soon to
a bookstore near you

Chapter 12

"Theron, please!" Kathleen shouted, and dodged the thrashing legs that threatened to shower her again with the clear water of the swimming pool. Theron shrieked with delight and renewed his efforts to drench his mother.

"You're a pest. Do you know that?" she teased, and grabbed his chubby body around the waist, lowering her head and nuzzling his neck while he strove to escape this show of affection. At seventeen months old, he was already developing an aversion to maternal protection and asserting his newfound independence. Only when he ran into trouble of some sort did he come to Kathleen seeking solace.

He was active, curious and headstrong, determined to have his way against all odds. On the days Kathleen was home, she spent nearly every minute in his company, basking in a glow of pride and love.

When Theron was born, Seth wanted her to quit working. He saw how time- and energy-consuming being a mother was. But Kathleen had been adamant.

"Before I was your wife, I was your employee. You hired me to do a very difficult job. Until I feel like I've accomplished what you outlined for me to do, I'll continue working at least three days a week. With the new store in Stonetown and the boutique in Ghirardelli's now open, you need me more than ever."

He acquiesced, but only if she would accept her current salary. Each week, she endorsed a paycheck and deposited it into a savings account. Seth wouldn't let her spend any of that money, but gave her a sizable "household account."

She had hired an assistant to help her, but was never far from the telephone when not actually in the stores or at her office.

Her assistant was a young man named Eliot Pate. He knew the retail clothing business inside out, had a flair for style and an uncanny instinct about what merchandise would sell quickly. They had recognized each other's talent, and an immediate friendship had sprung up between them.

They tacitly agreed to pretend that his unconventional love life didn't exist. He overlooked her flagrant femininity, and she overlooked his occasional bitchiness. When she was off, spending her days with Theron, she knew that Eliot had things well under control.

Today was one such day. She and Theron were languishing away the late afternoon hours in the Kirchoffs' pool. Kathleen never thought of this estate in Woodlawn as her house. It was too large, too ostentatious, and Hazel never passed up an opportunity to let Kathleen know who was mistress of it.

When Seth had first brought her here as his bride, Kathleen was intimidated by the apparent show of wealth, but gradually she had become accustomed to it, which was strange considering where and how she had grown up.

The traditional house was fashioned after those found in the English countryside. The lawn surrounded it in a broad expanse of green, perfectly clipped and trimmed. The interior was decorated with the most meticulous attention to detail. But to Kathleen, the rooms looked like settings in a magazine instead of where people actually lived. Hazel's personality was reflected in everything, and for that reason alone, Kathleen had never felt that she belonged here.

Her favorite rooms were those occupied by herself and Theron. Seth had generously offered to let her redecorate them to her own taste. She rid the rooms of the somber, cold, formal decor that Hazel had installed, and put in its place her choice of furnishings, which were lighter, brighter and much more conducive to everyday living.

Downstairs, what had once been a library had been converted into a den for Seth, which connected to a solarium that had become his specialized bedroom. Seth's den was cheerful and pleasant, and they often sat in it in the evenings, talking over the stores' progress and Theron's precociousness.

Now, as she bounced her child in the water, she marveled again at how well things had turned out. When she had married Seth almost two years ago, she'd had no reason to expect that she could be this . . . content. The word *happy* had almost formed in her mind, but that really couldn't describe her. Yet she felt a deep sense of satisfaction with what she had made of her life, when at one point it had seemed so hopeless.

Her relationship with the Harrisons had been restored. She had heard from them soon after letting them know of her marriage. Their congratulations were reserved.

But when she notified them of Theron's birth, she was deluged with presents and advice on parenting. Since then, they corresponded often and telephoned periodically, on birthdays and such. If that closeness they had once shared had cooled since that pivotal summer, Kathleen was at least glad that the lines of communication remained open.

She shared their happiness over Jaimie's adoption. When they told her about it, she felt only a momentary pang of jealousy for the family who had taken the boy into their lives. She often thought about the child who had touched her heart that summer.

With Seth's full endorsement, she continued as an absentee board member for Mountain View, making anonymous and sizable contributions to it. The checks were always drawn on an account Seth had in a New York bank and signed by his attorney. One, Kathleen specified, was to be used to build some tennis courts. For years, the Harrisons had wanted to add that sport to the summer curriculum. Kathleen tried to convince herself that her donations weren't made as recompense for the dreadful way she had treated the couple who had loved her so much.

Seth knew of the Harrisons, but not the extent of Kathleen's former relationship with them. He merely knew them as a couple who supervised a summer camp which Kathleen had attended when she was a child. She had never told him that she had been at Mountain View only weeks before coming to San Francisco. That subject was better avoided altogether.

The stability and peace of mind she was feeling this afternoon had been hard to come by.

"Do you want to go under?" she asked Theron. "Huh? Hold your breath." She sucked in her breath with an exaggerated motion, and then quickly pulled the small, sturdy body under the surface, only to bring it up again. Theron blinked his blue eyes and gasped for air, then crowed with laughter. He began bucking, indicating that he wanted to do it again.

Laughing, Kathleen said, "Hold your breath. Ready? Here we go." She dunked him again, and this time there was no delayed reaction. When he came up, he was already slapping his hands on the surface of the water.

His laughter and her own hoots of praise for his brave accomplishment prevented her from hearing Seth's van as it pulled into the driveway. Nor did she hear the sound of the hydraulic system lowering his chair to the ground, or the muffled voices as they came around the flagstone path toward the swimming pool.

"Kathleen! What's going on? We could hear you all the way on the front drive." Seth's voice, as usual, was warm with happiness. Keeping her full attention on her wet, wiggling son, she called over her shoulder, "Come see what Theron can do. He's very proud of himself."

"You be careful with that boy, Kathleen," George said from behind her. "He's getting almost too big for you to handle."

"He is at that," she agreed. Theron was now even more excited with his ardent audience, and waved his chubby arms at them before Kathleen told him again to hold his breath and dunked him under.

Everyone applauded when he broke the surface and smiled, revealing almost a full set of shiny white baby teeth. "That's enough for now," Kathleen said, laughing. "I'm pooped!" She lifted Theron out of the pool onto the redwood deck and he toddled toward Seth. George leaned down and picked up the little boy, swatted him affectionately on the rump and sat him in Seth's lap, disregarding the fact that his diaper was dripping wet.

Only when Kathleen turned around and walked up the mosaic tile steps out of the pool did she notice the other man standing quietly behind Seth's chair. There was something vaguely—

My God!

"Kathleen, I've committed the cardinal sin usually attributed to inconsiderate husbands and brought someone home for dinner without giving you notice."

Kathleen's heart was pounding so loudly that she could barely hear Seth's words as Erik stepped from behind the wheelchair. "This is Erik Gudjonsen. Erik, my wife, Kathleen."

Her heart seemed to swell and then burst, showering the universe with infinitesimal fragments of herself. And as it did, her world disappeared and was replaced by a smaller one comprised only of her and the man in front of her. Standing so close. Close enough to see, to hear, to smell, to . . . touch.

No, she mustn't touch him. If she did, she would die of the pleasure and the pain. But the decision was taken from her as Erik extended his hand. She watched that hand as it closed the distance between them. And then, almost in wonder at this miracle, she reached out and grasped it with her own, closing her fingers around it as though to verify that this was no dream, but actuality.

The gentle squeeze she received in return made it abundantly clear that he was real. Her eyes lifted from the studied attention she gave their clasping hands to his chest, over the firm, strong chin, past the sensuous mouth under that mustache which, even now, she fantasized about, along the slender, aristocratic nose, to his eyes, which bored into her.

There the exultant celebration in her breast was squelched. His eyes resembled pieces of blue ice, hard and unyielding beneath the shaggy, sun-bleached brows. Lying deep in their depths was a terrifying hostility.

"Mrs. Kirchoff," he finally said in acknowledgment of Seth's introduction. The world came back, righted itself and demanded that she behave according to custom.

"Mr. Gudjonsen." Her voice sounded foreign to her ears, and she only hoped that no one else noticed. His voice was poignantly familiar—deep, husky, befitting his size.

Then Seth was speaking excitedly. "Kathleen, Erik and I have been corresponding for the last several months. We're working on a project for the stores. I've wanted to keep it as a surprise for you. Now that Erik's here, we'll go over all the details after dinner."

Her smile was stiff, contrived, and she felt dizzy and nauseated, fearful that she might disgrace herself by throwing up at any moment. After the initial astonishment of seeing Erik here in her own backyard, feminine vanity had set in. She was all too aware of the wet hair that clung to her shoulders. She hadn't put on any makeup all day and was dripping wet, her apple-green maillot suit clinging to her shivering body.

"I can't wait to hear what you've been planning, Seth. If you'll excuse me now, I'm going to take Theron inside and clean him up before Alice gives him his dinner. I'll meet you on the patio in an hour for cocktails."

"Okay, but bring Theron back. I want Erik to see him when he's more presentable."

"He seems like quite a live wire," Erik commented as he looked down at Theron for the first time.

"Yes, he is," Seth said proudly. "You ought to see him try to negotiate the stairs. He's fearless."

With growing horror, Kathleen saw Erik peer down into Theron's face. The boy looked up at him with reciprocal interest.

"I have to get him inside," Kathleen said, and barged between Erik and Seth to pick up Theron. "Excuse me," she said as she held the child and hurried toward the house.

She practically ran through the kitchen door and, when she was safe inside, leaned against the wall weakly.

"Goodness, Kathleen, you look like you've seen a ghost. What in the world is the matter with you, girl?" Alice asked with concern.

Alice, George's wife, acted as housekeeper/cook and ran the house with the competence of a ship's captain. She was as soft and plump as George was hard and lean, but they complemented each other perfectly. Kathleen knew that the couple had lost a teenage son to muscular dystrophy. While Seth was still in the hospital after his debilitating accident, George had come to see him on behalf of a paraplegic association. He had offered his full-time services to Seth. The couple had been with him ever since.

Now, Alice crossed the tiled kitchen floor, wiping her hands on a towel.

"Oh." Kathleen laughed nervously. "I think I got too much sun. When I left the pool, I felt a little dizzy." She took a deep breath. "What's on the menu tonight? Seth brought E . . . a guest home for dinner. I hope that won't inconvenience you," Kathleen said, despising her breathlessness.

"No. I'd planned on roast beef, so it's already in the oven," Alice replied absently. She was more worried about Kathleen's pale color than how many people there would be for dinner. "I'll fix a fresh fruit compote for an appetizer, then serve salad and vegetables with the main course. Instead of a heavy dessert, what do you think of a crème de menthe parfait?"

"Sounds wonderful," Kathleen lied. The thought of eating was repugnant. "Well, Theron needs a bath."

"I'm sure he could use one," Alice said, laughing at the toddler, who was emptying a drawer of plastic measuring cups.

"Come on, Theron," Kathleen said, taking his hand and leading him out of the room. "If you need any help, Alice, call me." She always offered, but Alice never took her up on it.

"Don't worry about dinner. You just dress up pretty for the company."

Kathleen was glad that Alice didn't see her footsteps falter as she walked across the wide entrance hall from which the broad staircase rose majestically.

As she bathed Theron, her mind was spinning with a million questions she hadn't allowed to surface before. They did now. What was Erik doing here? What kind of business venture could he possibly have with Seth? Where had he been these past two years? What had he been doing? Was his wife with him?

He looked the same. No, he looked different. What was it? He was older. Time had etched tiny lines at the corners of his eyes. The creases on either side of his mouth were harder, less inclined to tilt mirthfully. His eyes—she shivered—his eyes didn't dance any more with devilish humor. They were cold, cynical, callous.

She placed Theron in his playpen and indulged herself with a bubble bath. *What was he doing here?* Why had he come back into her life when things were going so well? Why hadn't he come sooner?

She avoided the most important question, the one that plagued her more strongly than the others. Would he recognize Theron as his son? If he did, what would he do about it?

She toweled dry and padded into her bedroom with a bath sheet wrapped around her. Standing at her closet, she selected an ensemble, discarded it, then moved to another until she finally settled on a pair of white silk evening trousers. The accompanying strapless blouse was multicolored stripes in metallic colors. Her waist was swathed by a shocking-pink cummerbund. She slipped into white high-heeled sandals and put gold disks into her pierced ears. Two dainty gold chains encircled her suntanned neck.

Putting on makeup had never been so difficult. Her hand shook with the effort, and she smeared mascara that had to be wiped away before she could apply more. Since her butterfingers couldn't quite cope with intricate clips and combs, she decided to let her hair hang free and loose on her shoulders.

She had learned that in the Kirchoff household it was customary to dress for dinner. In the almost two years she had been here, she had rather come to enjoy that tradition. Besides, Seth liked to see her wear fine clothes.

When she was ready, she dressed Theron in a navy-blue playsuit with "Ahoy, there!" appliquéd in white letters on the front. As she brushed his thick cap of blond curls, she marveled again at the miracle of his birth. She had known before Dr. Peters had made the proud announcement in the delivery room that the child was a boy. Her early visions of him had been mystically accurate. She shuddered whenever she thought back to the time when she had contemplated abortion. What a tremendous sacrifice it would have been never to have known the joy of loving Theron.

Would Erik feel that affinity that she did each time she looked at Theron? Did fathers have that same oneness with their children that mothers did?

She swung Theron down from his padded changing table and took his hand. "Are you ready?" she asked, the question really directed to herself. The unqualified answer was "no." She was torn between her burning desire to feast her eyes on Erik once again and the anguish of seeing him dangerously near his son. But if she didn't hurry, Seth would wonder what was keeping her. She couldn't arouse his suspicions in any way. At all costs, she must remain cool and collected around Erik, for Seth must never know their former relationship. He must never be hurt. She prayed he wouldn't see the resemblance between Theron and their dinner guest.

They descended the stairs hand in hand. Kathleen slid open the glass door that led out to the patio, and, released from her restraining hand, Theron barreled past her toward the man sitting at the round, umbrella-shaded table sipping a drink.

Erik, taken by surprise, laughed and reached down to ruffle the curls on the head pressed against his knee. "Ahoy there, Captain. Where's your—"

At that moment, he glanced up and saw Kathleen standing in the doorway. *God, she's beautiful*, Erik thought, and impatiently swallowed the lump in his throat. He had considered himself cured, able to take anything fate threw in his path, but when he had seen her coming up out of that pool this afternoon, his heart sang with joy while his mind cursed the gods who had played this despicable trick on him.

From the back, he had thought the young Mrs. Kirchoff looked familiar. Her hair had a radiance that he had seen only once before. When she had turned around and he saw the face that had haunted him for years, he had ridiculed the desire that coursed through his veins like a raging fever, threatening to ignite him from the inside out until he disintegrated to ashes. Standing as she was, wet and glistening, time rolled back to another time he had seen her coming out of the water. He still had that tape of her. Only on the most depressive days did he indulge—and torture—himself by watching it. Today she had been no image captured on electronic machinery.

Somehow he prevented himself from vaulting past Kirchoff and taking her in his arms and devouring her with a mouth that was still hungry for the taste of her lips. But the other man was in the way. The man in the wheelchair. The man whom, over the past few weeks, Erik had come to admire and respect for his courage, integrity and shrewd business acumen.

Seth Kirchoff had talked about his wife endlessly, praising her talents and beauty to the hilt, but had he ever called her by name? No, surely not, or Erik would have reacted to that name. But who would have thought that Kathleen, *his* Kathleen, would end up as the wife of this San Francisco entrepreneur?

That was when his previous flare of joy at seeing her turned to bitter bile in his soul. Of course. She had run away from the struggling videographer when she had been given a golden opportunity. She had probably been disgusted with herself for allowing his hands to taint her. She obviously aimed for higher things. How had she felt about giving away her most valuable bargaining asset? It hadn't mattered to Kirchoff, Erik supposed, because she had gotten him to marry her. *Congratulations, Mrs. Kirchoff. You're a very wealthy woman.*

Seth had every reason to be proud of his wife, Erik thought as she crossed the patio toward him. She was lovely, graceful, motherhood having smoothed away some of her coltish angles and replacing them with feminine curves.

She was still slender, almost too much so. No one looking at her would believe that she had carried a child. Her stomach was flat, the results of fifty faithful and vigorous situps a day. If it weren't for the generous fullness of her breasts, no one would ever know that she was a mother.

Her heels tapped on the patio. He heard the rustle of her clothes as she knelt down to pick up the child at his knees. The silk covering her breasts gapped slightly and blessed him with a glimpse of the smooth, bare flesh beneath. Her fragrance wafted up to him as she stood. Passionate longing raced through his body and centered in his loins, making him throb with desire.

"Mitsouko," he spoke aloud, though he hadn't intended to.

Kathleen stood stock-still and stared at him. "Yes," she answered. Moving away from him, she took a chair across the table, keeping the boy on her lap. "I see you have a drink," she said breathlessly. She didn't look at him.

"Yes."

"Where is Seth?" she asked, almost in desperation.

"He went inside with George to change clothes. He said he'd be out shortly."

"Hazel?"

"Hasn't made an appearance." He took another sip of his drink and said, "So we're all alone, Kathleen."

Her head snapped up. He looked rakish in his crisp white shirt and navy blazer. The shirt was unbuttoned halfway down his chest and provided a view of the tanned column of throat and hard, hair-matted chest. Her fingers tingled in remembrance of how that hair felt over the contour of muscle. His beige slacks hugged the hard thighs and molded over taut hips and . . .

She raised her eyes quickly, hoping he hadn't noticed the direction of her gaze, but he had. He insulted her by tipping his glass in a mocking salute.

"I must congratulate you, Kathleen. You've come a long way from the camp counselor in the Ozarks. How long has it been now? Let's see." He squinted his eyes, feigning concentration. "Two years? Yes, two years. There was an accident at the airport in Fort Smith. It was costly in lives and equipment, but I managed to survive. It happened on July sixteenth at two forty-three in the afternoon." His tone was hard, intentionally hurtful, and Kathleen felt the tears swimming in her eyes.

"I'm glad . . . you . . . you survived."

"Yeah. Your concern at the time overwhelmed me," he said sarcastically.

What gave him the right to be angry with her? "I couldn't very well join the crowd around your bed, could I?" she asked tersely.

Crowd at his bed? What in the hell was that supposed to mean? There had been no one there except Bob and Sally, and she had never even met them. He had quizzed them enough to know that.

Before he could pursue her enigmatic question, George helped Seth onto the patio. Erik had noted that everywhere there were steps, ramps had also been built to accommodate Seth's wheelchair. Light switches and thermostats on the walls were also placed low so Seth could easily reach them.

"Well, I'm glad to see that you two are getting better acquainted. You look ravishing, darling." He wheeled over to Kathleen and she got up, setting Theron on the patio. Placing both hands on Seth's shoulders, she leaned over to meet his chaste kiss. He held her hands as she straightened. "Isn't she gorgeous, Erik? I'll bet you thought I was exaggerating about her, didn't you? Have you ever seen coloring like this, or skin so soft?"

Kathleen paled by several shades. Erik had seen much more of her skin than Seth ever had. Since he had brought her to this house, they had gone to separate bedrooms each night. He had only been in her room once, and that was when George had carried him up the stairs to see her completed redecoration. They kissed a warm goodnight each evening. But she went up to her room, while Seth went to his with George, who would get him into bed for the night.

"Your wife is indeed beautiful, Seth," Erik said, but Kathleen could hear the underlying mockery in his voice.

"George, would you please tend bar? I'll have a scotch on the rocks and Kathleen her usual spritzer."

Involuntarily, Kathleen's eyes went to Erik, who, unnoticed by Seth, again saluted her with his glass. They both remembered another time. Kathleen's recollections were warm. Erik's were obviously those of the triumphant seducer.